WYLDBLOOD

ISSUE 13 — SUMMER 2023

Wyldblood Magazine #13 - Summer 2023

© 2023 Wyldblood Press and contributors.
Print ISBN-978-1-914417-17-7

Publisher: Wyldblood Press, Thicket View, Bakers Lane, Maidenhead SL6 6PX UK.
www.wyldblood.com **Editor:** Mark Bilsborough. **Fiction editor** Sandra Baker. **Subscriptions:** 6 issues epub/mobi/pdf delivered to your inbox £20. 6 issue print subscriptions £35. Single issues available worldwide via Amazon and from wyldblood.com/shop

Submissions: we are regularly open for submissions of flash fiction, short stories and novels – check our website for our current status and requirements. We are a paying market. We also need artwork, people to review us, and people to review *for* us. Email contact@wyldblood.com

Issue 14 will be published in November 2023

Editorial

Summer's here so inevitably it's raining in England and a bit chilly. But what's going on with all those heatwaves further south? One of the downsides of reading so much science fiction is that we all know what happens next, and it isn't pretty, unfortunately. But hey ho, business as usual. Let's arrest Greta Thunberg for speaking her mind and dilute all our green pledges, eh? Short termism (and blinkered thinking) rules. Rant over.

In another part of the impending apocalypse we're not at Skynet yet but the wider world is beginning to wake up to the fact that AI might not necessarily have our best interests at heart, and while it may not yet have a heart, if and when it does, again, we know what happens next. Tricky little buggers, those (potentially) super intelligent beings. Maybe if we write some great stories about what might happen if we're not careful, we can *be* a bit mor careful. It's great that so many people working in the AI field have come out publicly and said 'woah'. But is it all talk?

But we in the writing and publishing world are noticing a few early warning signs. ChatGPT is, depending on your point of view, a wonderful tool for us to enhance our creativity (and quintuple our output – at the touch of a button or two) or, alternatively, the chill winds of an impending publishing apocalypse. The people that potentially lose out are the writers, of course (because increased artificial competition will squeeze them out and reduce rates), readers (because the stuff's not good enough yet, even though you've probably already read a ChatGPT article or story without realising that humans had very little to do with it). and publishers who care about writers (like us)– though plenty of others will in time see shortcuts and cost savings.

The better paying publications have seen a tsunami of AI generated submissions lately (less of an issue for us because we don't pay pro rates, though we've had a few), and despite everyone's best efforts it's not possible to say with any certainly that something is entirely (or even partially) machine generated. So the future is now and we have to live with it.

What does this mean for us? An uneasy feeling for now but I do think it suggests the little corner of the publishing industry we operate in is going to see profound change over the next couple of years. If we want to thrive we're going to have to live with that change, and that might be uncomfortable. But we're not prepared to compromise on our principles: (human) writers first and only. And long may that continue.

We've got plenty of human written stories for you to enjoy this issue: a new take on transferrable skills, a church that's very difficult to leave, sibling attraction that lasts a lifetime and more, a deal with consequences, little lies becoming long nightmares, alien entrepreneurship, a sacrifice for love, a love bringing sacrifice, Science fiction, fantasy and stories defying categorisation, all carefully selected to entertain you. We hope you enjoy them.

Mark

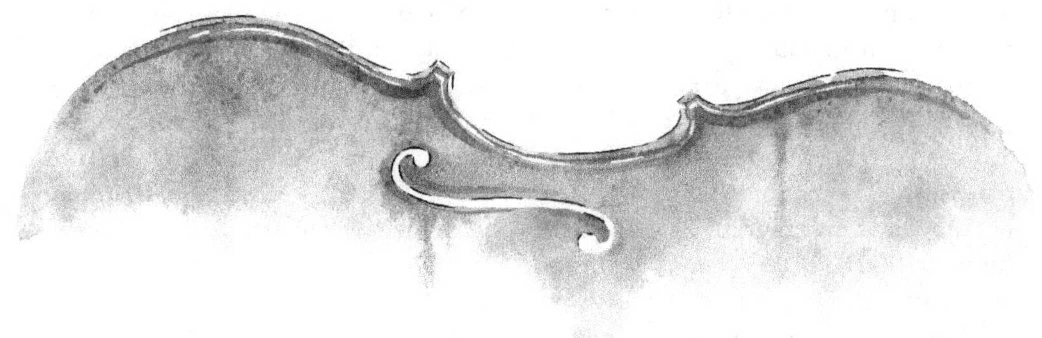

Skillset
Arlen Feldman

The violin player was a whim—something to take my mind off of my problems. I read an article about him in the paper, and watched a bunch of his concerts on YouTube. He wasn't even all that expensive—fifty grand to pay for his granddaughter to finish college.

He was so angry. But it wasn't as if he was ever going to play again. His Parkinson's was so bad that he couldn't even lift a bow. Still, the way he glared at me—like I was to blame for every problem in the world. It wasn't as if he was forced to take the deal.

I tried playing for the first time that evening, standing alone in my penthouse office. The violin felt natural in my hands, although the chin guard tickled the bristles of my five-o'clock shadow. I put the bow into first position, and it squealed as I ran it across the strings, making me wince. The angle was wrong. I knew that now, although I wouldn't have known it yesterday. I needed to get my brain out of the way. Closing my eyes, I tried again. The piece was the solo from Scheherazade, my hands and fingers knowing the notes, even though I'd never seen the music. It is

a beautiful piece, high and sweet, but somehow my playing of it didn't have the life of the old man's version.

Along with the ability to play, I now knew enough to tell the difference between the two different performances. They were both note perfect, but my version was dead. In some way, the old man had managed to withhold part of his skill. I sighed. This wasn't the first time that had happened. Some skills were so bone-deep that you needed more than just the know-how—you needed the heart behind it.

The first skill I had picked up was driving, entirely by accident, at age six. I was in the rear seat of the car, playing with a plastic steering wheel. My mother reached back to check on me, and suddenly I knew everything about how to drive a car—at least everything that my mother knew.

At exactly the same time, she lost all knowledge about driving and we ended up slamming into a tree. I was fine in my car seat—not even bruised. My mother didn't make it.

I generally don't drive if I can avoid it.

It wasn't until years later that I realized what had happened, and what I could do. I admit that, at first, I wasn't particularly discriminating. Back then, I took skills I wanted—skills that people had spent a lifetime learning—without asking and without any particular regret.

I rosined the bow and played some practice arpeggios. They sounded *okay*.

It took me a few years to grow up and grow a conscience. As you might imagine, with my abilities, I did well in the world. I resolved to never take a skill without permission. It wasn't that hard. A lot of people were good at things that they didn't particularly enjoy—a big stack of cash was often much preferred.

Although I have had more than my share of confrontations with people who changed their minds—or thought that it was all bullshit, and they were going to get a big check from some rich nutjob for nothing. Surprise—it was real!

One guy even tried to sue me—he was a barbeque champion. It never went anywhere, though—he couldn't convince the court that there was some sort of "skills vampire" out there. I'd used the opportunity as an excuse to learn the law overnight from an ex-judge, although the case never saw the inside of a courtroom.

It was kind of a waste though. What's the point of being a grill master when you have no one to cook for.

I tried the Rimsky-Korsakov piece again. A bit better, maybe. If I practiced, I'd probably be fairly passable. That was the problem, of course. I couldn't even count the number of skills that I *technically* possessed, but which required practice or ongoing education to keep up. Without continued application, the skills started to fade—just as if I'd learned them the normal way.

Not that I'm complaining. I've made several fortunes, and live a decent life. I stay relatively low-key, but I have a reputation for brilliance that is no less impressive for being, ahem, borrowed. And it isn't just the skills—I do work pretty hard. For obvious reasons I tend not to get too close to people, so I have a lot of time to fill.

My phone rang. I put the violin down carefully into its case before answering.

"Kyle Thomas?"

"Speaking."

"We know. You will pay." Just that, then the call ended.

I sighed. This was the ninth or tenth such call I'd received. The caller was different each time, as was the exact wording. This time it had been a man's voice, slightly gravelly. There had also been several nasty notes and a few break-ins—a slow, but steady escalation.

I made a mental note to inform my Head of Security. Not that it seemed likely to help—the security team had not made any progress on any of the other incidents or calls.

After the first call, my first obvious thought had been that someone knew about my ability, such as it was, and wanted revenge—perhaps from the days when I was younger and less fastidious about how I acquired skills. The funny thing, though, is that it might not have anything to do with that. I run a large company with fingers in a lot of pies. I had tried to instill a sense of morality into the company, but more than once we'd had scandals or had to fire a lower-level manager who didn't get the message.

The security team was theoretically looking into that possibility too. Another way to gain skills was simply to hire the right people—assuming they *were* the right people.

I picked up the violin again, but my hands were shaking and I made a complete hash of the piece. I decided to call it a day.

I took a taxi home. It was only about two miles to my apartment by the Park, and I usually walked if the weather was nice, but today I just didn't feel up to it. I tried to tell myself that it was *not* because I was worried about some sort of attack, but I was never great at lying to myself.

In theory, of course, I could defend myself. I had picked up several martial arts over the years, and had "learned" to shoot from an expert marksman. In practice, though, I was lacking—specifically, I was lacking *practice*. Martial arts require dedication to keep up. In truth, I was never very good, even though I had the skills of some true masters. My brain knew what to do, but my body did not. As for shooting—I never carried a gun.

So, taxi. I nodded at the security guard in the lobby, grabbed my mail, and then took the elevator to the top floor. I stepped into my apartment and into chaos. It looked like every single piece of furniture had been knocked over or deliberately destroyed. I had a few pieces of fancy glassware that had belonged to my mother—they had all been smashed. A wooden shelf was sticking through the large-screen television.

I stood staring for a long moment, numb. Finally, I made my way deeper into the apartment to see how far the damage went. It looked like it was everywhere. Even my bedding had been ripped to shreds and, as if there was some concern that I wouldn't get the message, painted above the headboard, in what I hoped was red paint, were the words: WE KNOW.

Only at that moment did it occur to me that whoever did this might still be in the apartment somewhere, lurking in wait. Just as the thought went through my mind, I saw a flash of movement out of the corner of the eye—but it was just my reflection in the jagged remains of the bathroom mirror.

I shook my head to clear it, then bolted for the hallway. The elevator was still on my floor, and I jumped in and hit the lobby button, then pounded on the close button until the doors finally shut. Only then did I relax slightly.

The security guard was horrified when I told him what had happened and he immediately got on the phone to the police. I knew that I should wait for them to arrive, but I needed air. The whole building felt stifling.

I pointed out the door. "I'm going to the Park. Tell them where I am when they arrive."

I could tell that the guard wanted to argue, but he just nodded. I pushed my way out of the building, crossed the road and walked to the nearest entrance. There was a bench about fifty feet away, where I frequently went to sit and think. I settled down and just breathed steadily for several minutes. It was only then that I realized that I was still carrying my mail.

Lacking anything better to do, I looked through it. Mostly junk and my water bill—for some reason, the water company seemed to have ignored the coming of computers and insisted on sending a paper bill every month. There was also my newspaper.

I was *just* old enough to prefer getting my news in print format, although I suspect that my sitting reading a paper in the park made me look a lot older than my forty-three years. The speckles of gray in my hair probably didn't help either.

I wondered a bit how long the police would take to arrive. For just a second the whole park seemed alien, and the handful of people walking around seemed like threats. I closed my eyes tightly for a few moments, and then opened them. It was just the park again.

In an attempt at normality, I tried to read the paper, although I found myself more skimming than reading. Politics was as crazy as usual—more so, since there was every possibility of a war breaking out because of some bizarre cloak-and-dagger stuff I couldn't be bothered to read about. There was an article headlined, *The Spymaster*, with a picture of a decrepit old man with painfully intense eyes. Apparently, this guy, Edward Latimer, was the one man who could have cut the Gordian knot of the international issues, but he was dying of cancer, and so we were all doomed.

I shook my head. I wasn't a big believer in the idea that any one person was so critical to the world that they couldn't be replaced. Although...the skills of a spymaster might be useful right about now. I grinned at the idea. Even with all of my random capabilities, that seemed rather ridiculous.

Heavy footsteps caught my attention and I looked up to see a policeman walking towards me. *About time*, I thought. I stood up, nodding at the man.

He was large, with a square face, his muscles bursting against a too-tight shirt. He didn't acknowledge my nod, and for a moment I wondered if he wasn't there to talk to me at all, but then he veered in my direction. He was probably annoyed that I'd made him come to me rather than waiting for him in the building. I resolved to be as meek as possible to try and make up for it.

"Hello, officer. I'm sorry I didn't wait for you, but..." I broke off when I saw the large knife in his hand. Before I could react, he plunged the knife right towards me. Some instinct, or perhaps some residue of my Kung Fu skills, made me flatten the newspaper and use it to deflect the thrust—barely.

I looked around desperately for help, but with that uncanny ability of New Yorkers to avoid trouble, the area around the bench was suddenly completely deserted.

I half-blocked another thrust, but felt sudden fire burn across my arm. I was a pudgy businessman fighting against a muscular killer who seemed extremely well trained in the use of knives. In a moment of intense clarity, I realized that I was about to die.

Then, out of nowhere, I got an idea. I did something that I hadn't done in decades—I reached out and took a skill without permission.

A look of confusion came over the cop's face. He was still holding the clip-point Bowie knife correctly, but I could see a hint of slackness in his thumb that hadn't been there earlier. Using a simple Pekiti Tirsia-style disarm, I removed the blade from his hand, then drove the blade towards the man's chest.

Then I stopped. It was obvious that this guy wasn't a cop, but even so, I had no interest in killing anyone. I'd taken away his knife skills and his knife. That should be enough.

But it wasn't. A huge beefy fist swung hard towards my head. I reacted automatically, with instincts I didn't have moments ago, moving, ducking, and striking all at once. The fake cop and I looked down together to see the knife protruding from his chest. Then he dropped as though all the bones had been removed from him.

For what seemed like an eternity, I stood there, staring. Suddenly there was a scream and, for a moment, I wasn't sure that it wasn't me.

It wasn't. A woman had come into the clearing near the bench and was pointing. Nearby, a kid was holding up a cell phone. How long had he been recording? Did he see me get attacked, or did he just film me stabbing someone that looked like a cop?

It was stupid, but I ran.

Have you ever completely forgotten about a song, but when you heard the first line, realized that you knew every word? Some of my skills are like that. A long time ago I'd picked up the skills of a private detective. I honestly don't remember why; it may have just been a whim.

Now that I was committed to disappearing, I had an automatic understanding of how to do it. The first step, which I'm pretty sure I would have figured out even without specialized knowledge, was to dump my blood-splattered jacket in the nearest trashcan. Rather more painfully, I also wiped my phone and pulled out and snapped the SIM card. They went into the next two trashcans.

Then I slipped off my glasses, slicked back my hair using water from the nearest water fountain, then casually sauntered through the Park in a more-or-less random way. I circled the reservoir, and headed generally towards the 96th Street exit. I hadn't been there before, but the part of my mind that *knew* how to avoid being followed also knew where to find a whole host of useful places, like thrift stores.

I emerged after twenty minutes sporting cargo shorts, an I *heart* New York sweatshirt, and a backwards Mets baseball cap. You would have to have seen me before to realize how radical a change this was from my usual suit-and-tie getup. I barely recognized me. I had my old clothes and several other new outfits shoved into an old backpack.

Fortunately, I tended to carry a lot of cash. When I'd first started out, I'd made a lot of my initial money playing poker—people didn't expect someone so young to have so much experience. Go figure. Although I didn't play often anymore, I still tended to carry a decent wad with me. At least I wouldn't have to worry about them tracing my credit cards.

I checked into a cheap hotel, and lodged myself in the hotel bar to think. For several hours I'd been running on automatic pilot, but now that my regular systems were kicking in, I was starting to shake. A beer, followed by a whiskey, followed by half of another beer were enough to calm me down, but also enough to make my mind a bit fuzzy.

The television in the corner was showing the news. I half expected the killing of a cop in Central Park to be the lead, but a potential declaration of war was still the top story. Small mercies—for me, anyway—less so for the country or the planet.

Now what? As I focused on the problem from the perspective of a detective, I realized that I'd made several mistakes. I should have searched the body of the fake cop for ID. Earlier, I should have called the cops about the threats so that I would be more credible when I tried to explain my side of events. Of course, my security team knew and would *probably* be believed by the cops. I should have gone to them, rather than running.

On TV, the detective always had one clue left to follow which led to the next one, and finally to the solution. I didn't have even that. A better detective might have had ideas, but the guy whose skills I'd acquired mostly knew about taking pictures of cheating spouses—and then hiding from said spouses.

My security team included ex-cops and FBI agents, and none of them had made any progress. So what chance would a two-bit private detective have? Even less, a two-bit copy of a two-bit detective? One problem with my particular ability was that I absorbed the skills of someone without really knowing enough about the skill ahead of time to know if the person was really as good as I thought. I'd been lucky many times, but unlucky just as many. I had been hoping for Humphrey Bogart, and got the peeping-tom version of Barney Fife.

I could, of course, try again, but these days I often spent weeks or months researching before acquiring a new skill. Even the violinist had taken a couple of weeks, from reading about him to finally meeting him. And *that* was a skill that was easily verifiable. Looking into serious investigators without any access to my systems or people—and then finding one who was in a situation where he would *willingly* give up that skill in exchange for something—the idea was ludicrous.

Just at that moment, the TV screen changed to show Edward Latimer, the spymaster, lying in a hospital bed. He looked ancient, with tubes running into him, but his eyes burned as he talked softly to the camera. I'm not a huge believer in fate, but at that moment it seemed like here was the one-and-only solution to my problems.

Funny thing was that I'd never heard of Latimer up until a few weeks ago. No one had, really. It was only when the world looked like it was on the verge of imploding that his name had come to the fore, and only then—it was suggested by the media—because he was no longer able to manipulate things behind the scenes.

Whatever the reason for his new-found fame, I now knew who he was and where to find him. My detective skills weren't up to much, but they were good enough to get me into a hospital room, even one with a guard. A brief stop at a uniform supply store got me a set of scrubs, and an hour at Kinkos got me a rough but serviceable ID. I twisted the cord so that it was actually the back of the ID that was visible—I knew from experience, albeit not my own, that almost no one would ask me to turn it back around.

A few hours later, I found myself walking confidently past a bored security guard, a bundle of bedding in my arms. And just that easily, I was in the hospital room of Edward Latimer.

The old man was sleeping, and I felt guilty waking him, but I had little choice. I had no idea how long I would have. I dropped my bundle of bedding, and reached out and gently shook his shoulder. He was so thin I could feel the bones through the thin cloth of his hospital gown, and I was afraid that even my gentle shaking might break him in half.

Eventually his eyes opened, and he blinked up at me then started coughing. I hastily pulled back my hand. He gestured vaguely towards a sliding table and, after a moment, I realized he wanted the water bottle sitting there. I grabbed it and held it for him while he sucked water through the built-in straw. Another gesture told me he was done, and I pulled the container away.

"Thank you." He squinted at me. "Mr. Thomas, isn't it?" he asked.

"You know who I am?" I took a step backwards, half-wanting to run.

He chuckled slightly, which brought back the cough. I leaned down with the water bottle, but he waved it away.

"For a while, you were considered a serious threat." His voice was so quiet that I had to lean close to hear him, but his speech was clear and precise. "Many of my colleagues wanted you locked up, but then you started acting a bit more responsibly. Though we never stopped watching you."

I had been so careful, I thought.

"Don't let it bother you," he said, as if reading my mind. "We watch a lot of people."

I didn't find this remotely reassuring. Latimer looked like some sort of shrunken wax doll, but I was suddenly terrified. And if I hadn't been in so much trouble, I think I would have bolted.

"So, what can I do for you, Mr. Thomas?"

"I...uh...I need help."

His eyebrows went up at this. I told him about the threats, the various acts of vandalism, culminating in the attack by the fake cop. When I was done, he just stared at me for what seemed like forever.

"You have a heightened belief in your own importance in the world, Mr. Thomas," he finally said. "I am lying here dying in a hospital bed. If I were not, then I would be trying to stop the world from catching fire." He had more to say, but started coughing again. The fit went on for a long time, but he waved away the water when I offered it.

I stared at my feet. I had a lot of guilt for things I'd done, but I'd never felt as bad as I did at that moment. The urge to turn around and just leave was strong — but my desperation was stronger.

"Mr. Latimer," I said. "Here's the thing. Maybe we can help each other. You aren't able to do your job any more, but your skills could help me figure out my problems. In return, I could do something to help you, maybe. I know you don't have much longer, but I'm very wealthy. Perhaps I could help your wife? Or your kids?"

It was a variation on my usual pitch, although I normally had a bit more data available — like the name of the wife and kids. I could tell from the amused look in his eyes that I'd blown it.

"I never had time for a wife or children. My parents are dead. I had a sister, but she's dead. She left no family. You don't have much to offer me."

I sagged, defeated. I could have tried a pitch about favorite charities or something, but I was pretty sure that wouldn't work either. I suppose I should have been proud of myself for the fact that, not once did the idea of taking his skills without permission cross my mind.

"Thank you for your time. I'm sorry for..." I didn't know what. I waved my arm vaguely around the room, then walked to the door.

"Kyle, wait." The voice was not much more than a whisper, but I froze. Perhaps it was the use of my first name.

"There might be something you *can* offer — something that I would be willing to trade."

The slight burgeoning of hope propelled me back to his bedside. I leaned over so I could hear him more clearly.

"How much do you know about what is going on right now? How close to the brink we truly are?"

I shrugged. "I've seen the news," I said. I knew the basics.

"Here is the deal I'm willing to offer you. You can have my skills in order to solve your problem, but in return—in return, you have to solve mine. Someone with my skillset, coupled with your other abilities, someone not stuck dying in a hospital bed, someone like that could solve this. Someone like that could stop us going over the edge. I am willing to trade *my* abilities for *your* oath to stop this madness."

"But," I protested, "I don't have your connections. I have no way even to get to the right people. Having the skills is one thing, but you know the players, the details."

"It will be difficult," he admitted, although there was a gleam in his eyes, "a challenge I would have relished when I was your age."

"But what if I can't do it—I can't promise…"

He raised his hand an inch or two, but even that effort seemed to exhaust him. He was barely even whispering now, although he still enunciated each word. "Okay, fair enough. I'll take your oath that you will do everything that you possibly can to stop this slide into chaos."

I closed my eyes and thought. Despite my successes, I had to admit that I hadn't really done much to help others. I mean, I gave a lot to charity, treated my employees well and all that, but I didn't pay that much attention to the world and its problems. If I were totally honest, I ignored everything around me and worked as hard as I did to avoid sliding into self-pity. But did I really want to get involved?

Then I pictured the fake cop falling to the ground, blood oozing around the wound in his chest. The wound that *I'd* caused. Did I really have a choice?

I opened my eyes, and looked directly at Latimer, trying to remember the exact words he had spoken. "I give you my word that I will do everything in my power to prevent us sliding into chaos."

He nodded slightly, satisfied. Then he steeled himself.

"Do it," he said.

I reached out and put my hand against his head, focusing on the skills I needed. It took longer than usual, felt different. For once, instead of feeling like I was stealing something from someone, it felt like it was being given—like he was forcing every last bit of knowledge and instinct into me.

And then it was done.

I pulled back my hand and waited for the new skills to settle in my mind. I could already see connections coming together—a clarity of thought I wasn't used to.

Latimer sighed and dropped further into his pillows, exhausted.

"Thank you, Mr. Latimer. Edward." I said.

He shook his head slightly. "Don't thank me, Kyle. Just fix this." He fixed his gaze on me, but it had already lost something—it was hazy, confused. "I'm sorry. I'm so sorry."

Then he died. It was as though he'd been holding on by sheer will power. Without the will, his body just gave up. His eyes went flat and waxy. Machines started beeping. I knew I only had a few moments to get out.

Instinct made me do a quick search of the room—an instinct I hadn't had a few minutes earlier. I found a briefcase in the wardrobe and grabbed it, then headed for the door. The guard was standing there, gun in hand.

"Cardiac Arrest," I said, gesturing behind me. "I'm going for the crash cart."

Then I walked briskly away, leaving the guard staring into the room.

It was an hour later, back in my hotel room, before I got a chance to go through the briefcase. It contained three separate folders. The top folder, by far the thickest, contained details of the crisis, along with lists of names and dates. I temporarily set that aside.

The second folder contained multiple IDs – FBI, CIA, NSA, several others. They all had *my* name and *my* picture on them. Kyle J. Thomas in black-and-white. I stared in horror for a second, and then burst out laughing. I already knew what would be in the third folder. It was now all so obvious.

The final folder held Latimer's plan. The attacks against me and my company, including the before and after pictures of the damage to my apartment. The specific steps to get Latimer's name out in the public where I would see it, after so many years in the shadows.

"Clever old bastard," I said. Still laughing, I returned to the first folder. I had a world to save.

As well as writing fiction, Arlen is a software engineer, entrepreneur, maker, and computer book author—useful if you are in the market for some industrial-strength door stops. Some recent stories of his appear in the anthologies Phantasmical Contraptions, Particular Passages, *and Kevin J. Anderson's* Gilded Glass, *and in* Little Blue Marble *and* Nocturne *magazines. He lives in Colorado Springs, Colorado. His website is cowthulu.com. Twitter: @arlenfeldman*

He Wants You to Stay
Thomas Nicholson

The smell of roast chicken and sunscreen blew through the car as they curved round a bend in the country road. Niamh let the wheel drift through her palms, keeping a close eye on the passenger seat. She thought Mary would have fallen asleep by now, but her friend remained determinedly awake, fingers working over the rosary beads dangling from her neck.

"Good to get some air, hey? Better than being stuck inside."

Mary didn't answer. She reached for the phone in her lap, touched a button on the side. The screen showed the same photo it had the past twenty times she'd looked at it. No new message covered either of the smiling faces.

"No news is good news, I guess." said Niamh, wincing even as the words came out. *Was there a more cliche thing to say?*

Mary stared out at the woodland surrounding them as if in a trance, stuck in torturous purgatory until either the phone rang to tell her what Niamh suspected was coming, or until they ended their trip and she trudged back up the hospital steps to Paul's bedside.

"Do you want the window up?" asked Niamh. "Not too cold, is it?"

"No. It's fine," sighed Mary.

"There's a blanket in the back. I can grab it if you want, or you can lie down there and I'll take the basket up here."

She was trying her best, but it seemed that keeping her mouth shut was the best thing she could do these days. She'd got enough practice. Even when Mary's husband was well, anything Niamh had to say about him had fallen on deaf ears. After the diagnosis, her suggestions had become a lot harder to make. She couldn't exactly call him a leech when he needed the assistance of two nurses just to stand up.

Well, if she couldn't offer her support in the ways that felt familiar, she could at least do something to take Mary's mind off her troubles. She doubted the poor girl had eaten a proper meal in days. The picnic resting in the back seat had taken all morning to prepare, but she would have made it every single day if she thought it was helping the slightest jot.

"I reckon we should just stop at the next layby. You must be starving."

Mary's fingers clacked, but no sound came from her lips. They drove on. There was little other traffic about, bar the occasional deer Niamh spotted in the trees. The fuel gauge was dipping towards the horizon, and when a sign at the next turn promised an eventual return to civilization ahead, she pulled the car into a narrow lane.

"So peaceful out here, isn't it? There must be somewhere we can set up."

The woods thinned on the passenger side, and after ten more minutes of pained silence, they saw their first indication of humanity for miles. A church, nestled a ways back from the road, behind a small car park. Mary's head followed the white wood door as they trundled past—the only evidence since they'd begun their trip that she could see at all.

"You want to stop off quickly?" asked Niamh.

"Would that be OK?" Mary's voice was quiet, but the mere fact that she'd spoken was enough for Niamh to turn the car around on the spot.

"Been a while since I've gone, but I don't think I'll burst into flames if I cross the threshold."

Mary's lips twitched. "Thank you. I'm sorry. I just need a place to think for a bit. Five minutes, then we can go."

They pulled into the car park. A smattering of other cars were sprinkled throughout the bays. Judging by the empty stretch of road in either direction, it was too far to walk from whatever village they'd left. Niamh wasn't sure what time Mass was; she hadn't attended since her parents stopped forcing her. Fingers crossed the priest, or whoever, would let her stand at the back while Mary did what she needed to do.

She might not remember the details of the church her parents went to every Sunday, but she was pretty sure it didn't look like this. Paint was peeling from the wooden panels. The gutters were filled with mulch, bowing in the middle under a steep sloping roof. Rust grew from the hinges of the door frame like bronze tendrils, spreading in all directions. Close up, the building looked less like a church and more like a barn. Niamh half-imagined that behind the door they would find a line of anaemic looking cows waiting to be bolted in the head.

The only thing reassuring her that her initial assessment of the building had been correct was the window. A huge stained glass piece filled most of the wall to the side of the door. She cocked her head to make sense of it. An arrangement of fruit sparkled in the centre, orange and green shards sitting in a black bowl. A pair of thick arms spread around the rim, but it was difficult to tell from the angle whether they were picking up or putting down more offerings.

Mary wasn't looking at the window. The hinges creaked as she pushed on the door. It shifted easily and she disappeared inside. Niamh gave the roof a wary look, then followed.

There were no cows to greet them. No priest giving a sermon, either. Just a few bare pews leading to a plain, wooden altar, split apart by the rays of light filtering in through the glass. Halfway down, she could make out a pair of heads facing away.

"Maybe we're early."

Niamh looked around for a font; she could do with a splash of water on her face, but nothing jumped out at her. No matter. They had plenty in the car, along with more than enough wine for communion.

Mary stepped tentatively down the central aisle between the pews, her shoes echoing off the stone floor. When she passed the two people, she inclined her head towards them. The weak smile she gave out did not last long as she pulled back and let out a gasp, clutching at her beads.

"What is it?" said Niamh, running to join her.

She followed Mary's gaze down to the couple. Never had she seen a pair of people looking so dishevelled. Even Paul at his worst didn't look like this. Their skin had the desiccated texture of old coconuts. The woman's scalp grinned up at her through her parting like a pale lip. The man's mouth was dry and dusty, like he might cough out a cloud of ash at any moment. Both stared ahead, towards the altar, unblinking.

"Excuse me," said Niamh. "Are you guys alright?"

The couple gave no indication they had heard her. Niamh looked at Mary.

"Are they...?"

Mary stepped forward, reaching out a hand to touch the woman's shoulder. As her fingers met the hem of her cardigan, the woman jolted. She let out a wheeze more shrill than the creaking of the door's hinges, shrinking away from them into the man's shoulder, which seemed to crumble in on itself as she made contact.

"Do you think we should call someone?" asked Niamh, once her heart had returned to its usual place in her chest.

"I don't know," said Mary. "Maybe. Yeah."

"Hold on, I left my phone in the car."

Niamh strode back up the aisle towards the door. There had to be a retirement community nearby. Or a charity that had brought the couple and forgotten to take them home. Someone who could come and help better than they could. For the first time in months, she wished they were nearer to a hospital.

A shadow moved by the window, and Niamh nearly fell as she staggered backwards away from it. A small boy stood in the low light coming through the stained glass, staring at her through wide eyes. He looked as surprised as she was at the presence of another person. His eyes flitted between her and the pews, his mouth shaking as if he was trying to speak.

"Is he OK?" said a small voice behind Niamh. Mary had crept up to stand beside her. She leaned forward so her face was nearly level with the boy's. "Are you with them?"

The boy nodded.

"Stay here," said Niamh. "I'll be two minutes."

She made to move towards the door, but the boy leapt in her way, blocking the exit.

"No! You can't!"

His voice cracked on the final word, piercing Niamh's ears. Free from the window's backlighting, she could more clearly see what he looked like. His hair was matted, and his dark t-shirt had several small holes in the front.

"It's OK. I'll be right back," she said. "I'm just going to get my phone."

"No!" the boy repeated. "Please. You can't. You have to stay here!"

He backed up towards the door, spreading his arms wide so they couldn't get past. Niamh felt a cold prickle on her neck. She was starting to remember why she had fallen away from the church in the first place. Too many weird men standing around in strange garb, watching her from hidden alcoves. Thankfully this boy was only young. She was not a big woman, but she reckoned she could get him out of the way, if she had to.

"Please. Just wait. It's not safe to go out. Mr. McKenna says if you do, if you…" The boy huffed and rubbed at his collarbone, clearly visible through the tattered t-shirt. "Please, he'll tell you."

Niamh and Mary exchanged a look.

"What do you think we should do?" asked Mary.

The boy was pressed firmly against the door. Judging by the look on his face, he was not going to move without a struggle. Niamh cursed silently to herself. All she'd wanted was a quiet day out to help her friend, and now she was weighing up the benefits of fighting a child. She had to make up her mind soon, though. The people in the pews looked like they might breathe their last any moment. Every minute they spent deciding might be the minute they slipped over from curable to too late.

While she was thinking, a creak split the ceiling above. The boy relaxed slightly. He mouthed *"Please"*, unable to make the sound any longer.

The creak came again, followed by footsteps. Niamh traced the dust floating down, watching the trail move from over their heads, towards the pews, disappearing as it reached the walls of a closed room next to the altar. The steps grew louder, and the door to the room opened.

A man emerged, dusting off the front of his wax cotton jacket and straightening the legs of his slate grey trousers. He did not look like any priest Niamh had ever seen. He looked like he'd just come from an allotment, like he'd spent the morning planting turnips and digging up stubborn weeds.

He stopped as he saw the three of them clustered around the door. The initial look of surprise on his face faded much quicker than the young boy's. It was not replaced with the welcoming smile Niamh had been hoping for, or the eager look of a priest given the opportunity to create a new convert. If anything, he looked worried.

"What happened here?" demanded the man. "How did they get in?"

"I'm—I'm sorry, Mr. McKenna" squeaked the boy. "I wasn't watching. I didn't…"

McKenna rubbed his face, his cheeks sagging low until his fingers released.

"Oh, James. What have I told you? You have to be more careful. Not everyone wants to come here. People have to know what they're signing up for."

"I know. I'm sorry."

McKenna closed his eyes, scrunching the lids tight. When they reopened, his voice was calm, as if the moment's respite had reset something in his brain.

"Don't worry. It'll be OK." He breathed in deeply, filling his lungs and expanding the chest of his jacket. "Nothing for it now, I suppose." He walked over to them and leaned on the back of the nearest pew. "I'm afraid I can't offer you any tea or anything."

"Have you seen those two?" asked Niamh, pointing at the couple. "You need to call a doctor."

McKenna twisted to follow her finger, nonplussed by the pair of fading bodies.

"Don't worry. They'll be fine. Everyone is fine here." He spread his hands. "Welcome to Oensted's Sanctuary."

Niamh looked to Mary for confirmation, for any indication that she knew who Oensted might be. A Saint her parents had mentioned that she'd forgotten about? An old Pope who'd performed some weird miracle?

"Sorry, father," said Mary. "I'm not sure I heard you. Oensted's…?"

"No need to apologise. And no need to call me father, either." He pushed off the pew, turning to take in the decrepit building. "Oensted's Sanctuary. Not many people have heard of him, but they should have. He was a blessed man. He came to this Earth to help those most in need, and help he did."

Niamh rolled her eyes. It was one thing to proselytise to a captive audience, but to do so when people might be in danger was something else. McKenna's tone bothered her. The fatherly lilt to his voice reminded her of Paul, of the patronising way he looked at her when she asked him if he'd thought about paying his wife back yet, like he knew far more about the world than she ever could.

"Right, well I think we best be off then. We'll let you guys take care of things here."

She felt the boy stiffen behind her. Mary did not seem to be listening. She was focused on the altar, her hand clacking.

"We can stay a few minutes, no?" she said.

Niamh stared daggers at her, but as she took in her friend, she could not keep up the look. She knew the deep lines carved into her forehead, the scars on her bottom lip from where she chewed it through the night, the quiver in her chin whenever she thought about checking her phone. These had all come out in force when she'd been wedged into the passenger seat of the car. In the dim light of the church, they receded into darkness.

"Fine. OK. A few minutes."

"Please," said McKenna, gesturing down the aisle. "Come with me. Make yourself at home. Step up to the altar if you'd like. Some people find they can hear him better the closer they get. Careful though. The steps aren't as solid as they used to be."

"You never thought of cleaning the place up?" asked Niamh. "Wouldn't old Oey-boy like that?"

McKenna smiled, the corners of his eyes crinkling. "We have quite a hard time getting new materials out here."

Niamh followed close behind as they made their way down the aisle, giving the people in the pews a wide berth. She sat in the front row, making sure not to let Mary out of her sight for an instant.

"What is it that makes this place a sanctuary, then?" she asked once McKenna had guided Mary to the altar. "And what did you mean *'what they're signing up for'*? We don't have much to donate, if that's what you're after."

McKenna took the seat next to her. He tugged up the pleats of his trousers, grunting as he eased himself down. "Truly, a wonderful man, Oensted. But, unfortunately, a jealous type. Maybe that's why he hasn't entered the stories so much." He scratched at his stubble and a sprinkling of white hair came loose. "No point sugarcoating it. Now you're here, you're here for good."

"Excuse me?"

Niamh folded her arms, her tongue shoved far into her cheek. *Oh, great.* She should have seen this coming. The lonely man in the rural church. He had no one but the very young and the very vulnerable to talk to all day. It was no surprise he wanted to keep them around. There were probably a hundred little thoughts floating around in his head that he was desperate for someone to listen to.

Seeming to sense the edge to her voice, McKenna shuffled away from her. "It's his blessing. All who arrive here will get what they need. He will even protect you from death, if you so wish. In return, all he asks is that you remain nearby."

Fabulous, thought Niamh. Just the sort of chat she was looking forward to this afternoon.

"And if we don't?"

McKenna let out a whistling note through his nose. "Whoever leaves his sanctuary shall suffer. That which they fear most will befall them, and they will deserve it, for shunning his grace."

"Oh, fuck off." The curse echoed around the room as Niamh stood up. "I'm going to get those two some water."

A hint of guilt flushed her face as McKenna winced at her words, but she didn't stop. There were better ways to spend her day than listening to crap like this. She made it to the door in a handful of long strides. The boy, James, was still standing there. He had slackened when they moved away, but now he braced himself against the mouldy wood once more.

"Look," said Niamh, "If you let me past, I'll get you anything you want. I've got crisps, chocolates, whatever you fancy. It's all in the back of the car right there. Thirty seconds, and you can have it. Deal?"

James looked tempted. He licked his chapped lips, shifting from foot to foot. For a moment, he looked like he might step aside, but then Niamh heard McKenna getting to his feet and the boy snapped back to his guardpost. With surprising deftness, he reached behind his back and the lock clicked.

"Thank you, James," said McKenna over her shoulder. "You can go now. Check on Alfred for me. He was looking a little rough this morning."

Niamh turned to see McKenna standing in the aisle. He at least had the decency to look repentant for the bullshit he'd spouted. Although that did little to make her feel better.

"You can't go any further than the front door," he said. "He will punish us too for those we let leave. We must stay here and rely on what we have. He provides for us, and we are grateful."

The anxiety that had been building in Niamh's stomach could not lay dormant any longer. Swearing at him had gone someway to masking it, but the click of the lock like a gun cocked and loaded made her insides burn.

"Don't be scared," said McKenna. "You're safe now. It's a hard world out there, but in the Sanctuary nothing ever goes wrong. Take me. When I got here, the place was empty. No one cared for Oensted, but he showed me the way. I got on my knees at that altar and he spoke to me." McKenna's eyes flicked to where James had disappeared into some dark corner of the room. The whites swam and roiled when he couldn't find him. "He told me this is my duty. There was nothing out there for me anymore, but if I served him, I would live in peace and harmony. And I have. If you stay a while, you'll see too. You'll want to stay. And as long as you do, he will keep you whole."

At this, Mary looked up from where she knelt at the altar, head bowed.

"Is it true? Can more people come here?"

"We don't advertise. Not everyone wants his gift. Some prefer to find their own path, but, yes. All who arrive enjoy his protection."

Niamh's stomach clenched so hard she could have sworn she'd been punched. Fanatics were always dangerous, and McKenna's voice sounded so sincere she had no doubt he believed what he was saying. She had never come close to that level of belief in anything herself. Paul might as well have been in the ground as soon as Mary told her what the doctors had said. She wasn't like her friend, still holding out hope that he would pull through. Mary had given him so many chances in the past, always believing that this time things would be different. How might McKenna be planning to exploit that belief? How might he abuse it?

She edged back to the window while McKenna's attention was on Mary, eyeing up the glass. She could try and smash her way out, but the panes looked too thick, and what if she slashed an artery? No one was coming to save her out here, not if she couldn't get to her phone.

The glass looked different from the inside. Green and orange light danced on her flesh, but she could see other colours too. Black and grey veins ran through each shard. The fruits did not look ripe or juicy anymore, but rotten. Huge hands hugged the bowl tight, connected to arms that led up to the top of the glass, to shoulders that surrounded a wide chin receding into the ceiling.

Niamh breathed slowly. No point going to pieces. McKenna clearly wasn't all there. She had to get out, one way or another.

"Mary?" she called.

Mary was back at the altar, her face almost touching the wood. The wrinkles on her forehead had deepened, as if she were concentrating hard.

"Mary?" Niamh called again.

This time Mary frowned and looked up.

"What?"

"Are you done yet?"

"Just… Give me five more minutes, OK?"

She returned her attention to the altar, and Niamh bit down hard on her lip. OK. Fine. She was going to have to do this by herself. She would find some side door, get her phone, and come right back. Easy.

She put on her best smile, the smile she was used to faking anytime she was out with Mary and Paul together, and fixed it on McKenna. Best to play along for now. Don't risk riling him up. He looked a good few years older than her, but she knew better than to underestimate the strength hiding under that jacket. Unlike James, there was no way she'd be able to do anything if this fully grown man turned violent.

"Well, I guess we're staying then." She nodded at the couple in the pews. The woman's head had sunk into her partner's chest. "Might as well make ourselves useful. Anything I can do to help?"

McKenna's eyes softened, seemingly relieved by this change in attitude.

"There's a leak in the roof we use to collect water," he said. "I already bottled enough to drink for today. If you could collect some to mop their faces. It's been a while. Just, please don't go outside. You'll understand soon enough. Just give it time."

"Sure thing. Where's this leak then?"

He pointed to the room he'd emerged from.

"It comes down the back wall when it rains. Feel free to use the sponge. It's clean."

Niamh nodded. "You gonna be OK there Mary?"

She hadn't expected a response, so when none came she did not let her nerves take over. Instead, she walked calmly to the door McKenna had pointed to. A desk sat in the centre of the room, backed by empty bookshelves covered in dust. What looked like a nest of blankets took up one corner. Was this where McKenna slept? Looking at the ragged pile made her nervous, like something might rise up from their depths to drag her in.

The leak ran down from the ceiling, pooling in a bucket at one corner of the shelves. Niamh barely looked at it. Something far more interesting took up one wall. A staircase, winding up to the floor above. She tried to remember how the building had looked from the outside. Was there another window? Somewhere she could climb out, roll down the tiles, and drop near the car?

She nudged the door closed behind her and tested the bottom rung. It did not creak. Likewise, there was no noise coming from the main room, no indication of what McKenna or Mary might be doing, might be talking about. Niamh glanced at the door, then grabbed hold of the bannister as she took the next step. Damp wood pressed into her palm. Nails sticking out of the slats rattled as she put her weight forward, and she let go.

She had to duck as the staircase twisted and the room above came into view. More an attic than a room, in truth. She had been expecting some sort of belfry, even though from outside she could not remember seeing any. Instead, she was met with a triangular roof held up by sagging beams.

The knot in her stomach loosened as she registered the strip of light running through the centre of the uneven floorboards. A circular window had been cut into the wall at the opposite end. Treetops rippled through the smudged glass. Her heart jumped in her chest. She had to go. Now. Before McKenna guessed what she was up to.

She started forward, but her toe caught on something hard lying on the floor. She threw out a hand to stop herself from falling, grabbing onto a support that looked like it was just about holding the roof up. It took everything she had not to cry out, to risk them hearing her below.

She flexed her aching toe, looking down to see what had obstructed her passage. Just like the one she'd found by McKenna's desk, half a dozen piles of blankets lay untouched by the strip of light. They looked to have been arranged into two rows, the closest of which started right in front of her.

She could not hold in the gasp of surprise as the pile moved.

Not a lot. Barely an inch, but she was so close she could see every shifting square of fabric. The topmost blanket rose and fell rhythmically. Further back, others were doing the same. Like ancient bellows working a dying forge, whimpering grunts gurgled through the room. The blanket at her feet twitched as it felt her touch, falling away to reveal what lay underneath.

A pair of sunken eyes stared upwards as if she wasn't there. The skeletal bridge of a nose sniffed like it could sense her, but did not move towards where she stood. The head looked almost too small to be human, like it had shrunk in the wash. Skin stretched tight over bone. The ears had shrivelled to tiny shells. But it was alive. Breathing. Like McKenna had promised. Protected. Safe.

"What are you doing up here?"

The voice made Niamh spin on her heel, and she grabbed the support so tightly she worried it might rip free. James crouched over one of the piles she hadn't seen behind her, further from the window.

"James…" she said. "What is this? What's going on?"

The boy ran a hand over the blanket in front of him, soothing the nest's occupant.

"They came for his blessing, and he gave it to them. Mr. McKenna says they'll be safe. As long as they want."

"Did he... did he bring them here?" Niamh asked in a whisper, terrified of how far her voice might carry.

James frowned. "I—I don't know. They were already here when we came."

The boy looked even more frightened than when he'd held the door closed. His lank hair hung over his eyes, and in the crouch his threadbare trousers had pulled up above his bony ankles, naked feet shivering on the floorboards.

"How long have you been here?"

James looked at his hands, counting on his fingers, then gave up and shrugged.

"OK. Don't worry. We're going to get you out. You and your family. Please, just stay quiet."

"No!" The word came out in a squeak and Niamh cast a nervous glance to the staircase.

"Please, James. Please be quiet."

"No. I have to tell Mr. McKenna. You're not allowed to leave. He said."

"McKenna's not in charge of you. You don't have to do what he says." James shook his head. "No. Not him. Not what *he* said. He keeps them safe. Please, don't hurt them. He won't like it."

"I'm not going to hurt anyone. I want to help."

"They already have help!"

Niamh shut her eyes, breathing through her nose. Alright. She wasn't going to convince him. He was too brainwashed by the zealot holding him hostage. A different tack, then.

"OK. Fine," she said, taking a single slow step backwards towards the window. "We'll keep helping them here. It looks like you're doing a great job. I'm sure Mc— I'm sure *he's* very proud of you." She waved a hand slowly in front of her face. "It's so stuffy up here though, isn't it? I think these people could use some air. I'm just going to open the window for them."

James looked warily back, but did not move to stop her. Niamh continued towards the window, shuffling her feet to avoid stepping on any more blankets. She imagined dust loosening onto McKenna's head. She couldn't afford to take her time with this. Not when he might dash up the stairs at any moment.

She felt the sun's heat on her back through the glass. The gap was small, and higher than her waist. She would have to jump up and shuffle through. Turning slightly, she could see the car park in the corner of her eye. It wasn't that big a drop. Fifteen feet or so. She could do it. She could make it.

In one movement, she turned away from James, grabbed hold of the window, pushed it open, and bent her knees to spring. The creak of a floorboard made her hesitate for just a second. She tried to launch herself up, but she didn't seem to be going anywhere.

A harsh snap made her look down. One of the floorboards had cracked and given way. She could see the front door of the church through the hole left behind. James let out a yelp, and before she knew it, he was on her, pulling at her, trying to drag her away from the window.

"We have to stay!" he shouted. "We have to!"

Small, powerful fists nipped at her sides. Sinewy arms tried to fasten around her ribs, and she had to struggle to stay free of their grip. She kicked out and heard a shriek of pain as her foot connected with something soft. The arms fell away and she lunged for the window. Her fingers touched glass. She tipped. Fingers grasping.

Her foot would not move. Stuck in the hole left by the missing board. The top half of her body lurched, while her bottom half remained resolutely stiff, trapped, as if the church itself were holding onto her. Her shoulder connected with a roof support. Splinters flew, scratching her face as the wood split.

James was somewhere to her left, coughing and spluttering, but even that noise couldn't cover the complaints coming from the ceiling. She froze, clinging desperately onto the windowsill. Then the world disappeared in a cacophony of cracking, buckling sound. Niamh was twisted round, battered by wood and stone as the roof caved in. The floorboards were ripped away, flung in all directions. She saw the roof, then the floor, then the sky, until she hit the ground with such force that her lungs emptied.

Her vision tunnelled. A hard edge was stabbing at her hip and her right arm had gone numb. She tried to sit up, but the world tilted too far. Two figures swam ahead of her, growing larger. Mary and McKenna, both open mouthed, both trying to speak. The words did not make sense to Niamh, as if she were hearing them from underwater.

She managed to turn her head enough to see what was around her. The ceiling was gone, replaced by grey clouds high above. A section of the front wall had collapsed. The giant window had shattered; shards littered the dirt around where she sat, outside the remains of the door. James lay on his back, eyes fixed on the clouds as if he were staring at the headlights of an oncoming train.

Niamh turned back to see McKenna's face filling her view, covered in dust and filth like he'd crawled out of a coffin.

"Oh my… Are you—"

He reached out as if to help her up, then recoiled. *No surprise there*, thought Niamh. She stumbled to her feet on legs like water. Distance had become difficult to judge all of a sudden. The two figures swirled in and out of focus. Mary was within reach, if she could just grab her. Niamh tried to reach out a hand to pull her towards the car, but her arm refused to move, dangling useless at her side.

"Come on!" she wheezed, her lungs on fire. "Let's go!"

Mary stayed where she was. She looked to McKenna for reassurance, but he did not seem in any state to give it. His head shook slowly as he grabbed a clump of thinning hair.

"Oh my… Oh no…" he mumbled. "Oh—"

Any further comment he might have had was cut off as James collided with his hip, wrapping his thin arms around McKenna's middle. He ran on tiptoes as if the dirt outside the church was lava, burying his face in the man's jacket.

"I'm OK! I didn't go outside! I didn't mean to. I promise. She did it. It wasn't me."

McKenna let go of his hair to hold the boy in his arms.

"It's alright. Shush now."

"I'll be OK, won't I?" James sniffed. "I only went out a little bit. He won't be angry, will he?"

Niamh's head was ringing, but she wasn't about to waste the opportunity. With her good arm, she grabbed Mary's sleeve and pulled. She felt resistance, but not enough to stop her. Mary soon gave in, allowing herself to be dragged across the threshold. Neither of them looked back as more thuds and bangs shook the ground. Niamh thought she heard McKenna shout, but her ears were too full of the sound of the church falling in on itself to work out what he might be saying.

"Are you OK? You're not hurt?" Niamh asked as she threw herself into the front seat of the car.

"I— No. No, I don't think so," said Mary. She reached for the beads around her neck, but seemed unable to find them. Instead, she began picking at her nails. "Niamh, what did you do?"

"It was an accident. I was trying to get out through the window."

With one arm, she tugged at the wheel, reversing out of the car park back onto the narrow lane.

"Did you hear anything up there?" asked Mary.

The shrunken face swam through Niamh's mind, the sniffing of that wasted nose.

"Oh yeah. I heard something alright."

Mary turned to look at her. "Really? I thought it was just me."

"You—what?"

"At the altar. I thought I heard something."

"It was probably me and that kid. When I tried to get out, he came at me. Little git."

"Oh. OK."

Dust flew up to cover the windows as the car bounced over potholes. Niamh gave the church one last look. The top half was exposed to the world like an open wound. Blankets blew in the breeze, unpeeled plasters revealing a dark trench. The ground floor was a mess of debris. Wooden beams covered the entrance like police tape, criss-crossing over the space where the door had been.

She could see James and McKenna in the doorway. As she watched, McKenna guided them further inside, his arm still wrapped around the boy's shoulders as they disappeared into the ashy smog.

"You're bleeding," said Mary, nodding at Niamh's arm.

Niamh looked down to see a green glass shard sticking out of her arm like a shark's fin.

"It'll be fine," she said. "We'll sort it later."

"Why did you do it, Niamh?"

"I told you. It was an accident."

Mary shook her head. "You shouldn't have done that. We were supposed to stay there."

Oh for Christ's sake. All the months of frustration bubbled to the surface at once. All the times she'd tried to bring Mary out of her funk, all the times she'd spent hours raising a smile, only to see her friend's eyes darken as she trudged back to that waste of space at the end of the day.

"You were gonna stay there forever, were you? You were gonna give up on Paul to go play make belief with some lunatic living in the woods? Get a fucking grip, Mary!"

Niamh squeezed her hands around the steering wheel. Maybe that was too far. She could see the rest of the day play out before her. Mary would clam up, staring out of the window. They would spend the next hour driving back to the hospital. Then she'd go home alone thinking of all the better things she should have said instead. Later that night, Mary would call in tears and she would be there again to comfort her.

"I heard something," said Mary. Her voice was not the usually mousy whisper. There was an edge to it that Niamh didn't recognise. "It wasn't you. I know it. He told me. He said everything was going to be OK. And for the first time in a long time, I believed him. If I'd just stayed… Now we're gone, I…"

Niamh leaned forward so she could see through the windscreen to the dark clouds above.

"Look. Sky hasn't fallen in, has it? We're alright. Nothing bad is going to happen."

The adrenaline of the fall was wearing off now and the pain was setting in, a dull ache making her arm throb. The ringing in her ears was deafening. She shook her head to get rid of it, but it refused to go away.

"Can you hear that?" she asked.

Mary reached down to the side pocket of the car. When her hand returned, she was holding her phone. The screen glowed bright, and Niamh looked away as the light stabbed her eyes.

"Who is it?"

Mary raised the hand to her ear. Her cheeks had drained of the last touch of colour left in them, and her fingers shook so badly she nearly dropped the phone as she answered the call. Voice stolen once more, she mouthed a single word.

"Hospital."

Thomas Nicholson is a UX designer from the UK who has spent time living in Spain, Colombia, and Vietnam. His short stories have appeared in anthologies and magazines around the world, including publications from Guilty Crime, Sonder Lit, and Scare Street. He has previously been shortlisted for both the ITT Tallaght Short Story Prize and the Crossing The Tees Literary Festival Short Story Competition.

Three Dead Sisters
H.V. Patterson

Raw grief propels me, dazed and reeking of sour sweat, back to my hometown after twenty years of absence. As I sleepwalk into the funeral home, I think only of myself, bereft without my sisters.

I stare down at Bella's body. She's beautiful and serene, like Snow White, like she'll wake at any moment. But this isn't a fairy tale. When I reach out and squeeze her hand, it's cold and limp, the flesh slightly giving and redolent of embalming fluid. It was her heart, the medical examiner said, a defect long suspected. Just like Aurora.

In the next room, everyone pities me. I can practically hear them saying: is she next? Is she like her sisters, her death cradled behind her ribs, nestled inside a defective ventricle?

I don't cry. Maybe I've spent too much time with dead bodies. I teach high school biology, and I lead dissections for my classes several times a semester. There's a place of detachment which transforms a body into a tool for learning, for finding the truths hidden beneath the skin. The mortuary does smell like my classroom on dissection days: formaldehyde, a cloying-sweet scent of chemically masked death.

Bella is wearing a pair of hideous black pumps she hated. I pull them off without thinking, exposing her purpling toes. Her sky-blue nail polish is chipped in places, and her second toes are longer than her big toes—Morton's Toe is the technical term. All three of us inherited it from Mom. There's something so vulnerable about Bella's dead toes. I reach out and cup them in my hands.

That's when everything changes.

I'm wearing Grandma's iron ring, the one she gave to me thirty years ago as she lay dying. A bit of the cold iron to keep me safe from witchcraft and enchantment, to help me see through glamors and spells.

When the ring touches Bella's foot, her dead flesh ripples before my eyes and becomes wood.

I jerk my hand back, and the foot is flesh again: cold and dead.

I touch the ring to her skin once more, and it transforms into wood.

Grandma's stories flit through my head, and a strange, wild hope swells my heart. But I can't jump recklessly to conclusions. I must be sure. There are wire cutters in a nearby drawer. I don't know how they came to be there, like a left-handed gift from god, but I don't hesitate. I line the cutters up and snap them shut.

Bella's left pinkie toe comes off easily, plinking against the dingy tile floor. I pick it up and turn it over in my hand. It's not a toe at all: it's a carving of a toe. Green sap drips into my palm, and the room fills with the fresh scent of pine. It's exquisitely done, the carving, clearly made by a master, by someone with centuries to perfect their craft.

I look at the rest of Bella's foot, but nothing's changed. It looks like a corpse's foot, minus a toe. The glamor on this false body, this carved effigy of my sister, is strong. But Grandma's iron ring has revealed the truth, and that's enough to shatter my world and challenge everything I ever believed.

I shove the pumps back on and make my plans.

That night, I visit Aurora, my younger sister, who died when we were teenagers. Northern White Pines, some hundreds of years old, surround the small graveyard where she's buried, and fawns drift out of the trees in the summer to feed on the flowers adorning the graves. It's a peaceful, quiet place, one I haven't visited in twenty years. Near Aurora's grave, there's a freshly dug hole waiting for our older sister, Bella.

Books and movies don't show you how hard it is to dig up a grave, especially when you're alone at night and you can hear things moving just outside the invisible, consecrated line that separates the graveyard from the rest of the world. Inhuman creatures lurk at the edge of graveyards, but they can't walk on hallowed ground.

Rage, grief, and the most terrible emotion of all–hope–keep me moving the shovel up and down, even when I can no longer tell the difference between my sweat and my blood. Whenever I wonder if I should stop, if I'm losing my mind, I press my wet fingers against the wooden toe in my pocket to center myself, turning it over and over like a worry stone.

Bella's corpse is fake: Aurora's must be, too.

I picture Aurora as I dig, her honey-brown hair, her warm, brown eyes, the goodness she radiated. She was so sweet and beautiful, but Bella and I never resented her like older sisters do in fairy tales. We'd included her in all our games. We'd looked suspiciously at every boy who talked to her, caught in the golden net of her hair.

Behind me, an eastern screech owl's cry cuts through the night, and the rustling sounds continue. I don't bother to turn and look; I know I won't see those who stalk me from the trees until they're ready to be seen. I concentrate on keeping my bloody hands moving.

Eventually, the hole gets so deep that I have to clamber to the bottom and start tossing soil up. Half of every shovelful rains back on me, coating my face and hair with grave dirt. But I keep going.

Again, I conjure Aurora's laughing face, the slight gap between her front teeth, the way she always lit up the room. I remember the three of us running across the dunes and crashing into Lake Michigan during the summer, the shock of the icy water soothing our sunburnt skin. How can I still miss someone so much, all these years later? My grief is still raw, a wound that refuses to scab over and heal.

My shovel clangs against the lid of Aurora's coffin. Slowly, I sink to my knees, arms and shoulders aching. How many hours have I been digging? I look up at the blanket of stars, the sliver of moon above me. I teach my students a little about astrobiology, but we know so little about the stars and what dwells in those vast, open spaces. We don't even know everything lurking on our own planet.

I wrench my gaze down again. My palms are scraped raw. There must be hordes of bacteria teeming in the wood handle of this old shovel, flowing freely into my blood. But it feels right, the red drip from my body into my sister's grave. It reminds me of Grandma's stories: blood and sacrifice.

I brush the dirt off the coffin lid. The revealed wood gleams obscenely. My mother might not love her living daughters, but she spares no expense for her dead ones.

I wait for the tears to come, but they don't. Instead, my dependable hands reach out with the same clinical detachment that propels me through dissections. It's a split-couch coffin, designed so the top-half can open during the wake. I still remember Aurora's face, peaceful and asleep, coated in more foundation than she'd ever worn in life. I brace myself for whatever lies resting inside my sister's coffin. As I pause, memories of Aurora's death, of what came after, rush over me:

#

Twenty Years Ago: Aurora is dead, and I'm a walking wound. After the funeral, Bella flees with her own pain, back to college, swearing never to return. All at once, I'm not the middle sister, held and comforted: I'm just another girl, alone, sleepwalking through school. My house fills with my mother's weeping. She silently hates me for living. I want to reach out, to weep with her, to tell her that I also wish it were me buried beneath the sleeping fawns at the edge of the woods, but she won't let me. Her grief is a wall between us.

And then, the dreams start.

Every night, I dream of Aurora. She's outside my window, tapping playfully on the glass. She's dancing in the yard, flitting in and out of the woods surrounding our house, her laughter seeping through the walls. I wake up sobbing, my heart breaking all over again.

In my dreams, she gestures for me to come, to step onto the dew-kissed grass, to take her shimmering hand. But I never do. I watch from my locked window, my heart in my throat, but don't dare go outside. For months I dream, letting the final days of high school slip through my fingers like sand. My eighteenth birthday comes and goes with a sigh. I plan my move to Colorado for my first year at CU Boulder, but none of it feels real.

Suddenly, it's my last night in my childhood bedroom. Everything I own is in my car. Tomorrow, I'll begin driving across the country. The moon is full and swollen with the promise of a future, endless years without Aurora. Eventually, I fall asleep.

The dream returns. Aurora knocks on the window. This time, I climb outside. We walk in silence across the yard into the sheltering trees. I run my hand over rough bark, the ground cold and unforgiving beneath my sock-clad feet.

"You're going away," Aurora finally says. "You're abandoning me, like Bella did."

Aurora's eyes are luminous. Behind her, shadowed by branches, something shifts and writhes.

"You left first," I say. "You died. And Bella's gone. I can't stay in that house with Mom."

"But I never left. I've been here all along, waiting for you. Come with me!"

Come with her? Buried in the ground, my face rendered chemically serene? I shift away, pressing my back against a tree.

"Will you come back? To visit?" she asks coaxingly, like I'm a feral cat she's trying to lure indoors.

I press my hand against the bark again, marveling at how real it feels. I consider lying, but I force myself to tell her the truth. Dream or no dream, I've never lied to my sisters before, not about anything important.

"I don't know. I don't think so."

"Then this is goodbye." She looks away, and her face catches the faint moonlight filtering through the dense branches. "I wish I could cry. I see you and Mom cry all the time, but I can't anymore."

I reach out, closing the distance between us. She buries her face against me and is completely my sister again. She smells like lavender body wash and Herbal Essence shampoo.

"Do you remember Grandma's stories?" Aurora asks. "About the Fair Folk?"

When we were little, Grandma told us that the Fair Folk had followed our ancestors to America, and we must always be careful not to cross them or get their attention. Because if you caught their attention, they'd either kill you or take you, and either way you'd be lost to the human world forever.

"I broke the rules," Aurora confesses.

This close, it's impossible not to notice that her pupils are too big, and her chin is a little sharper than it should be. She smiles, and the gap between her front teeth is gone. It's like someone ran a filter over her, correcting every human flaw. This dream is too real. I fight hard against my unease, against a sudden, sharp desire to run.

"You didn't break any rules," I say.

"I must have," she insists. "I must've done something to get their attention."

I don't remember exactly what happens next. I think I tell her a story about three sisters crashing through the woods, disregarding the path, disdainfully flicking away ticks, laughing at the bright, open world. Three sisters screaming as they jump into every stream and lake, fearless of leeches, fish, and creepy men. These three sisters caught the attention of the Fair Folk. How could they not? In the story, we three sisters are powerful. Sister, protecting sister, protecting sister. Hand in hand in hand.

I don't remember how the story ends.

When I wake the next day, my body aches, and my feet are covered in mud.

In the graveyard, I shake off the memories and finally open the coffin.

Aurora's serene face is as perfect and untouched by decay as it was twenty years ago. She's so young. The three of us had felt so old and wise when we were teens, but we'd just been kids. I laugh, a hollow bark that doesn't echo. If this were a different kind of story, Aurora's eyes would open, her mouth would widen into a smile accented by sharp canines, and I'd chop off her head and put a stake through her heart.

I press my ring against that beautiful, youthful face. The glamor fades. Seconds later, I'm looking at a wood effigy of Aurora sleeping.

In our Grandma's stories, the Fair Folk sometimes took a liking to a particular person. Maybe they were beautiful, talented, smart. Maybe, like Aurora, they were all three. Sometimes, they'd take a piece of wood and make an exact replica of the favored person. They'd take the real human and leave the copy. Mom found Bella, seemingly dead in her sleep of a heart complication, two days ago. Twenty years earlier, I'd found Aurora, cold and dead in her bed. It'd seemed like an eerie coincidence, a tragic quirk of shared biology.

But the truth is: my sisters aren't dead.

"Rose," calls a voice from the woods.

My heart lurches. I'd thought she was alive, but it's a different thing entirely to hear her calling me.

I feel like I blinked, and half my life flew by, like I haven't been fully awake, fully aware of my life and all its potential, since I was seventeen. Three sisters became two, and I'd lost myself. Is it like this for everyone? Do most people dream their lives away, nursing hidden griefs and secret pain?

I climb from the grave, but I don't turn toward the voice. Not yet. The night is a welcoming cloak of velvet around me, the moon burnished silver, full and waiting. Everything is still.

"Rose, turn around."

My breath hitches in my throat, and I obey.

Aurora and Bella stand at the edge of the trees. Their dresses are spun from leaves, bark, and stray fragments of stars. They're young and alive in the pure, fierce way I remember being, back when we were three sisters, unafraid and indivisible.

My cry shatters the silence around us. I fall to my knees. Rage, loss, and love war inside me.

"How could you?" I scream. "How could you leave me all alone?"

All these years of feeling incomplete. All these years alone, sleepwalking through my life.

"We're the ones who left," Bella says. "We're the ones who fled where she couldn't follow."

I can't look at either of them, alive and yet separated from me by a barrier as insurmountable as death. Instead, I look at my ruined hands, my palms scraped to rags, my swollen knuckles.

My hair is graying, the corners of my eyes are spiderwebbed with wrinkles. I feel ugly and mortal before the creatures my sisters have become.

"We're here now," says Aurora. "We'll never be parted again."

I look up. Fireflies dance around them. Behind them, dark shadows move and twirl in a restless dance. If I focus on the shadows, I know I'll see things with sharp smiles and sharper appetites. But I only have eyes for Bella and Aurora. Love shines from their perfected faces.

"Why are you here?" I ask.

"To take you away," Bella says. "We've missed you so much."

"The three of us need to stick together," Aurora says. "Sisters should stay together. No matter what."

I rise and walk towards them. The scent of pine grows sharper. There's something at their feet, a stiff shape the size of a person lying in the dirt. When I get closer, I see by the light from the hovering creatures I mistook for fireflies that it's a perfect effigy of me.

"You know what to do," Aurora says. She and Bella push the figure into the graveyard, their hands never straying past the protective barrier of trees.

I stare at my feet, perfectly mimicked in wood, the index toe jutting out longer than my big toe. I feel a rush of tenderness for my feet, imperfect and human, which have carried me for so long.

I put Bella's toe and Grandma's iron ring in Aurora's coffin. They've served their purpose, and I won't need them again. Despite my exhaustion, it doesn't take long to refill Aurora's grave.

Wood should be heavy, but my effigy is light, easy to maneuver. I place it between Aurora's grave and the hole that will hold Bella's false body. When they find me tomorrow, they'll think my heart gave out from grief, and they'll bury me between my sisters, exactly where I belong.

My effigy looks sad and lost, her wooden eyes seeing nothing. Is this how I've looked my whole adult life? Have my students seen this emptiness in my face as I lecture about cell biology? I stroke my effigy's forehead, wishing someone had comforted me all those years ago. My blood soaks into the wood, and the glamor activates. The wood ripples and becomes an exact replica of my cold, dead flesh, the lines of grief and worry around my mouth and eyes softened at last. I press one of the cold cheeks. It gives softly, smelling of death.

"Sister?" Aurora calls.

I survey the tableau before me. One covered grave, one open grave, one body.

What will it be like for Mom to find all three of her daughters reunited in death? I know I should care, but whatever love I had for her evaporated years ago. There is only wild joy.

"Coming," I call, turning toward the woods. Around my sisters, fantastical shadows twist and writhe. I hear the Fair Folk whispering to me, welcoming me in a language I'll soon understand.

I walk forward, focusing only on Aurora and Bella. They wait just beyond the hallowed ground, arms open to receive me.

Sisters belong together.

I step into the woods. Cool pine needles brush against my face. Loving fingers tangle in my hair. My sisters are alive and well, and I embrace them.

Sister, protecting sister, protecting sister: hand in hand in hand.

H.V. Patterson (she/her) lives in Oklahoma. Her poem, "Mother; Microbes" was recently selected for the inaugural Brave New Weird: The Best New Weird Horror, Vol. 1 forthcoming from Tenebrous Press. Her speculative poetry and short fiction have been published by Sliced Up Press, Creature Publishing, Horror Tree, Dread Stone Press, Shacklebound Books, Penumbra Online, and Etherea Magazine. She promotes women in horror through @Dreadfulesque on Twitter and Instagram. Follow her on Twitter @ScaryShelley.

Bark and Skin
Madeehah Reza

When she closed her eyes as she brought the flask to her lips, Dushka could smell the ocean. Her nose prickled with the smell of brine lapping over seaweed and the faintest glimmer of charred lobster. She could almost forget that she was an old woman sitting in a dark room.

The syrup swirled as she gently shook the flask, the glow of the liquid dappling her skin with deep blue waves. There was just enough left for one last drink. Cool air rushed down her limbs like frost over a field. It settled at the tips of the bark before all that remained was a gentle breeze at the periphery of her skin.

She lit the oil lamp and dragged out a small table from beneath the desk. It had a large groove in the middle. Dushka lifted her right leg into the groove and traced a finger from shin to knee. Fresh bark covered her leg like a thick carpet. Stiff roots emerged from the soles of her feet, gnarled and dry. At the edges, where skin met bark, were traces of gleaming ocean blue. She gripped a chisel and mallet and took a deep breath before biting down on a ball of cloth. This ritual never lessened in its pain of parting. The old woman's cries rang ceaselessly, echoing through the cottage and across the forest floor.

An hour trickled by. Dushka took the rag from her mouth, soaked in saliva and tears, and cast it across her bloodied foot. It would heal quickly, perhaps even before the next hour, but it frightened her to look at the grisly thing. A layer of sweat slicked her forehead. The old woman laid back against the chair and steadied her breathing. Long shadows danced across the walls as the oil lamp flickered in the draught. Pain convulsed through her leg but Dushka ignored it. She reached over with a grunt and held the flask up to her eyes. She knew all too well this ritual of distracting herself, to tide over the injury. A dribble of syrup remained at the bottom of the flask.

Once, on a night like this by a crackling fire, Papa had taught her how to make the strange medicine. He'd shown her how to grind the ingredients that were fresh from the ocean floor and boil them down until they were pure enough to mix into a thick syrup. Papa made potions and elixirs for every ailment that washed over their little village by the sea. Dushka would sit by her father as he worked tirelessly into the night, never telling her off for her stream of questions. He would throw his head back in laughter, his smile broad and warm, showing the gaps in his teeth like pebbles in yellow sand. But this was many hundreds of years ago. Before Papa became sick.

Crimson seeped through the bundle of cloth. She wiped the sweat from her face with the back of her hand and tied the rag tightly around her foot before setting it carefully on the floor. Then, she rested her left leg on the table and examined it.

All bark and little skin.

The old woman panted as the midday sun beat down on her face. The forest awakened around her; a chorus of blackcaps and willow warblers echoing in sweet unison. Dushka preferred to travel when she could see the path ahead of her as it was said that when night fell, ancient relics of the forest shaped the trees anew.

Though her skin had returned to its normal sandy brown, calloused and cracked, an aching throb gripped the heels of her bare feet. She clutched the handle of a wicker basket in the crook of her arm as she stumbled over a fallen tree trunk. Water rushed just beyond the thicket. A flowing river splintered into shallow streams that fed the forest and town, with half a day's journey in between them. The town wasn't much farther from here, but the old woman's legs begged for a break. She perched on a large rock by the riverbank. In faded memories long since buried she remembered a wish made by this river. A request, an arrangement, a deal. A curse that had no cure.

A small creature scuttled at her feet, its body hidden beneath the hem of her skirt. Dushka smiled as she bent down.

"Ah, Delphi. Come to see this year's gifts?" She removed the white linen cloth over the basket. Inside were dozens of figurines, carved smooth from her bark. She plucked one from the pile and presented it to the field mouse. He sat on his hindlegs on the rock, whiskers twitching as he examined the figurine.

"Do you like it?" she asked, turning the carved piece in the morning light. It was a wooden mouse with a vacant expression peering at her. Dushka wished she could have painted it, to bring it completely to life, but her stores of paint and dye had long since gone.

The real mouse squeaked for attention.

"I know. You are, of course, far more handsome."

Delphi placed a tiny pink paw on Dushka's hand before he crawled up to her wrist and tapped gently on her skin.

"What is it?" She pulled up her sleeve. Woody vines wound around her wrist and spread thickly to her elbow. Delphi looked up with ink drop eyes and tilted his head. Dushka pulled her sleeve down and put the mouse back on the rock.

"And what would you have me do about it? We both knew this was going to happen."

She broke a stale piece of bread in two and placed the smaller piece on her lap. Delphi shook his whiskers and scurried off to sit on her shoulders.

"I do hope you're not this fussy when I'm no longer around," she said, though she chewed her piece reluctantly. She closed her eyes and listened to the steady stream of the river, like a dozen voices speaking over each other, words and water overlapping. How different it was to the vast call of the ocean.

"You're meant to have regrets at my age," she said softly. "But I don't regret this, not for a minute."

The mouse remained quiet. Dushka gently stroked Delphi's small head on her shoulder.

"Though cutting off all this bark is rather tiresome, don't you think?"

With each visit to the town the old woman always stopped outside the bakery. The roasted scents of fresh breads and sweet pastries filled the air as she peered through the window. A tall, thin boy with a pimpled face placed freshly baked goods on the display. He glanced up at Dushka but did not return her smile. Instead, he walked away with the empty tray swinging in hand. In the reflection of the glass, the old woman saw her puckered smile disappear.

Dozens of warm pastries lined the display: soft bread rolls, golden poppy seed muffins and slices of powdered apple strudel. But what caught Dushka's eye was the tower of pastry balls at the centre. Pink petals sprouted from its crevices and melted chocolate topped each pastry. A sheen of caramel came down the tower, like a golden-brown waterfall, and ended in a nest of spun sugar.

"A dessert fit for a king, don't you think, Delphi?" But the mouse was nowhere to be seen.

A soft blow hit her on the back. Dushka stumbled before she saw a tattered ball at her feet.

"Hey, kick it over here!"

A few yards away, in the centre of the empty town square, stood two girls and a small boy. The tallest girl waved both arms at Dushka. The brown-haired boy pulled on the girl's sleeve before whispering in her ear.

"It doesn't matter if she's old!" she exclaimed. "She can still kick a ball."

Dushka lifted the hem of her skirt. The tips of her toes were stained a russet brown, the soles of her feet already beginning to harden. Papa's medicine was not strong enough to quell the curse this time.

"It's that lady!" said one of the girls. "She comes every year."

The children gathered around her before Dushka could kick the ball back to them. The boy frowned at her, his little nose wrinkling and creasing a face full of freckles. "What lady?"

The shorter girl, with raven dark hair tied up in two tails, snatched the ball away from the old woman.

"Don't you remember?" she said. "She always comes at this time of year and gives us these little presents."

"I don't remember that!" said the boy.

"Because last year you were a tiny little *baby*."

"I'm not a baby!" the boy wailed, but the girls ignored him.

The tallest girl's sharp black eyes narrowed. She kept her head high as she eyed the basket in Dushka's arms. "You gave me a fox last year. I didn't like it."

"And why not?" said Dushka, her aged voice scratchy and sore. She placed a hand inside the basket. The girls took a step backwards.

"I don't like foxes. They *steal* things."

"And I wonder what the foxes might say about you, in their little dens?"

The tall girl scowled as she placed her hands on the boy's shoulders. "Mum always said you were strange," she muttered. "Let's go."

"But what about the presents?" said the boy.

From beneath the linen Dushka pulled out a small wooden rabbit. It sat on its haunches, large ears drooping at the sides.

"Here you are." As she placed the carved animal into his small hands, the older girl slapped it away.

"Sara!" said the raven-haired girl. "Don't be so rude!"

"She's *a stranger*, Asha. We shouldn't even be taking this stuff from her!" Sara snatched the ball back and stormed off. She dragged the whining boy away by his hand. Asha stooped down to pick up the rabbit. She blew the dust on its head before handing it back to the old woman.

Dushka shook her head. "You keep it for your friend."

"He's my little brother, actually."

"Is that so? Then here, take this one for yourself." She produced the wooden mouse from the basket. Asha appraised it in her hands with a hesitant eye.

"I've never liked mice. They're always getting in the way in our house. And Mum screams whenever she sees one."

"Then you should meet my good friend Delphi. He's lovely company and never gets in the way."

Asha gave a small smile as she clutched the wooden creatures. "You live in the forest, don't you? We always hear screams from there." She fell quiet, as if in thought, before she squinted at Dushka's head. "You have some leaves in your hair."

Dushka patted her head and found the foliage. She tried to tease them apart from her silver locks but the stems pulled at her scalp.

"Asha, come on!" yelled Sara from across the square. The dark-haired girl smiled once more before running to her siblings, rabbit and mouse cradled in her arms.

Dushka dangled her feet back and forth in the river as the ripples glittered golden in the sunset. Time had slipped away from her like water running through her fingers; it left a cold sensation, but nothing else. She'd sat for a whole day in the square and watched as families and children and small blackbirds went about their business. For so many years she brought her gifts to the town and children would flock to her for a little wooden creature. Now, her unwanted animals lined up on the riverbank in a small orchestra. As night slowly settled in the sky, a faint blue glow shone from the small cracks in their bark. Like tiny guardians they watched over the river, standing sentry at the edge of the forest.

The town had changed since she first made her journey to it. The bakery had been the postmaster's office; a few doors down was the wash house; a lively marketplace spread across the square where she had bought her paints and dyes for the figurines. It was all gone now as people moved closer to the cities, away from these smaller towns with few amenities and even fewer jobs.

She dragged her fingers through the long, wild grass of the riverbank. The bark had settled between her knuckles and the ridges of her fingers. When she moved, Dushka could feel a coarse and rigid husk encasing her. Papa's medicine only kept the burden away for so long, and now there was none left. If she closed her eyes she could remember his face, his warm eyes, his greying hair, but she wanted more than a memory.

In the flow of water, Dushka watched her reflection undulate at her feet.

What an odd thing I've become. A strange, melted portrait.

Three hundred years prior, beneath a moonlit sky, she stood by this riverbank as she searched for help so far from the ocean. It was said the spirits that lived in the forest held old magic that could revive even the dead. Papa forbade her from seeking such a solution.

You cannot find healing from those creatures, he'd told her before she left their cottage. *My dear, the difference between a cure and a curse is but one letter.*

But Duskha wouldn't listen to his ailing voice and instead had placed a kiss on his wrinkled forehead.

On the other side of the bank sat an ancient creature. Its ugly face was a cluster of twisted roots and pulsating vines, its mouth a hollow crack. Dark purulence leaked from the corners of its mouth.

"You are not a child of the forest, are you?"

The creature had several crooked limbs and used four of them to dip itself into the river.

"Are you a river spirit?" she asked. It waved another limb lazily in the air. A writhing appendage was attached, like a grotesque hand with many long fingers.

"Why are you here, child?"

The girl did not probe further.

"My father is sick." Fear crept in between her words. "Papa is all I have left in the world, and I don't know what I would do without him."

The ancient creature crawled closer still, water rushing past its shrivelled body.

"And you seek a cure for your dear Papa?"

Dushka sat on the wet, slippery river bank and dangled her legs into the water. The pull of the water was strong, so she gripped the long grass tightly.

"The healer says there's no cure," she whispered.

The beast stood in front of her. It surrounded Dushka, shrouding the moonlight.

"Perhaps there is a way to deliver a cure," said the creature.

Dushka's grip on the long grass loosened. "Yes, anything."

Dark liquid oozed from the beast's mouth as it towered above her. "My, you *are* beautiful. Will you give your beauty in exchange for your Papa's health?"

Dushka frowned. This was not what she expected from an old, wise spirit. She tried to move away from the creature that encroached on her space. "What has my beauty to do with anything?"

"Everything has a price," said the creature.

She stood up and moved away from the edge of the river bank. "My *beauty* is not for sale."

The creature came closer, its wet limbs crawling out of the river. It placed a shrivelled hand on Dushka's face. "But what will you do without your Papa when he is gone?" Its long fingers stroked her cheek. "All alone in this world."

She grabbed one of the fingers and bent it backwards until there was a *crack*.

The creature screeched; Dushka let go and ran away before slipping on the floor of the river bank. She fell against the ground. A cold sensation wrapped around her leg before she was dragged into the water.

"Foolish girl," snarled the creature.

Dushka heard little else as the water filled her lungs.

Delphi lay nestled in a crack in the old porch. Dushka sat down beside the mouse with a large sigh, her aged body aching all over.

It was not easy to go through the pathless forest in the dark, and she had torn her skirt somewhere along the way. There was a time when she would have looked over her shoulder at every whisper and snap, frightened of unnamed beasts and spirits. But all creatures die, even if it takes hundreds of years.

"Isn't it just so nice to sit down after a long day!" she said to Delphi. "And where did you disappear to?"

The mouse squeaked and raised its paws in protest. Dushka laughed. "Fine, you're off the hook."

She closed her eyes and leant against a cracked pillar, fidgeting until she felt comfortable. "It's all changed so much, hasn't it? I remember when the town was filled with people. There was a big market, do you remember? And a stall that sold the most wonderful bread."

Delphi did not squeak back. "Don't tell me you've scarpered off again—"

A small figure appeared from the shadows of the clearing. Dushka made to stand up, to move or defend, but her feet were sewn to the ground. Fresh roots twisted and turned at the soles and sunk into the soil.

"Who are you?" she called out sharply. "Make yourself known."

The figure came forth, the shadows dissolving into the dark-haired girl. Her eyes were round with fright, shoulders hunched. She carried a wicker basket with a linen cloth.

"It's me, Asha!" she said, her words wobbling.

"It's not safe to come out here on your own, girl."

"I… I just wanted to know who you were." Asha edged forward until she stood a stone's throw away from the old woman. "I brought you something from the bakery."

She reached into the basket and pulled out a small package wrapped in brown paper and stained with grease. It wasn't the king's tower of pastries or a poppyseed muffin but a squashed slice of sweetened bread.

"Sammy, the baker's boy, said you were staring at the display this morning. I couldn't afford the nicer stuff, but… well, here." Asha offered the opened package to the old woman. "I'm sorry about my sister this morning. She's always telling us to be careful with strange people."

The roots had found a stream of water hidden deep in the soil. A coolness spread from Dushka's feet and up through her limbs, like a fair breeze on a warm day. The old woman took Asha's offering and stared at the cold slice of bread. Her mouth watered on command, like a wild dog that hadn't eaten in days. The girl nearly dropped the basket in horror when she saw the small branches in place of fingers.

"Your sister is wise to warn you," said Dushka. "Does she know you're here?"

Asha shook her head. "We all know to stay away from the forest."

"Then why are you here?"

"I was getting ready for bed when I saw the mouse you gave me start glowing. I went to find my brother's rabbit…" she trailed off as she looked guiltily at Dushka, "…alright, I never gave him the rabbit! I wanted it for myself. But I saw it was glowing as well." Asha placed the basket on the ground and dropped to her knees, emptying its contents in a hurry. "I had a strange feeling that if I didn't come to the forest tonight, I wouldn't find you at all. I didn't know where I was going because it was so dark, but I found these by the river!"

Placed in a line were Dushka's wooden creatures, each luminous with a deep ocean blue. Asha placed her mouse and rabbit at the end of the line. "The closer I came to you, the brighter they got."

The old woman stared at this gathering of creatures—a squirrel, a hedgehog, a tiny owl and more—carved from her skin and laced with the potion of her father. Blue light dappled across the ground and washed against the trees, drowning the forest in the ocean's depths.

Dushka took a bite of the bread. It was hard to swallow with such a warm lump in her throat.

"You should go home," she muttered."

"But who *are* you?"

"No one. Just a very tired, very old woman."

Asha sat cross legged on the ground, a smile on her round face. "I thought you might be really old. Even Granny remembers seeing you when she was a little girl, and she's nearly eighty!" She paused as her gaze caught the old woman's lower half through the tear in her skirt, already thick in a dead layer of bark. "Why are your feet like tree trunks?"

Dushka couldn't bring herself to say the word. "I was searching for a cure."

Asha flinched when Delphi scurried towards her. "Oh, it's your mouse friend!"

Dushka could not find the right words. She ate the rest of the bread. The girl allowed the mouse to scamper up her arm. "What was the cure for?"

"My Papa," said Dushka. "He had a terrible illness that no doctor could heal. I'd met a man learned in magic in this very forest. He offered me a cure, a way to bring my Papa from the brink of death.

But this man wanted things in exchange, terrible things, and I refused to give him anything. When I tried to run, he cursed me."

"I thought only wood spirits and river demons lived in the forest," said the girl.

Dushka looked into the dense thicket, watched as shadows moved around the clearing of her cottage. "No," she said simply. "There are only men in these parts."

"And your Papa?" asked Asha, her mouth a sad line.

Dushka's head felt heavy, as if it was weighed down by something sitting on top of it. Leaves bristled in the breeze at the edges of her vision. The old woman closed her eyes and watched as Papa sat next to her, his mouth curled in a tired smile. She smiled back, placing her small hand within his rough palm and kicked her feet in the warm, glowing waves in front of them.

Madeehah is a pharmacist and freelance writer from London, She writes short stories and creative essays and has recently completed an MA in Creative Writing. You can find more of her work through Twitter: @madeehahwrites

$20
Richard Zaric

I hold my breath. There's a twenty dollar bill on the ground near the tomatoes. Its bright sheen stands out against the stark, white floor. It's a Saturday morning and the grocery store is busy but I happen to be the only one in this aisle.

I quickly scan the area. Shoppers are everywhere in the produce section, just not near the tomatoes. Anyone could have dropped it. I bend down and pick it up. It's a nice new crisp one with no folds or creases. Again, I look around. Nobody is checking their purse or frantically searching the ground. Whoever lost this twenty doesn't realize it. They might not even be in the produce section anymore.

What luck! How often is it that you stumble upon a twenty? Never! My heart starts racing. I slip the twenty in the pocket of my jeans, take a deep breath and walk away. I switch the basket to my other hand to pull out my phone to check the time. Better hurry. I still have to clean the washroom and vacuum before Maxine comes over.

After grabbing a pack of carrots, I turn to head for the dairy section and bump into an old lady.

"Sorry!" I say.

She only manages a faint smile. Her face is lined with more wrinkles than a Tarantino movie. The faint wisps of hair on her head likely turned grey over forty years ago. Her twisted hands could be used to teach the effects of arthritis to medical students. The very definition of a crone.

She narrows her eyes and purses her lips. Her slow nod drips with annoyance. Jeez, I said I was sorry. She turns and heads towards the lettuce.

What is it with old people in grocery stores when it's busy on Saturdays? The seniors shuffle slower than plate tectonics. They sometimes stare at a shelf for minutes. Are they contemplating a particular product on the shelf or are they thinking back to some random event that took place 50 years ago? No one knows for sure. They could shop at any time during the week, but they *have* to go on a Saturday.

I pick up hot dogs and buns. Pretty sure the mustard is low, so I throw a new bottle in my basket. I'm standing in the 12-items-or-less checkout when I realize I forgot to get a couple onions. Damn, I was just about to put my stuff on the conveyer belt.

Back in produce, I'm picking through the lose onions when I notice Robert Bearens. I haven't seen that guy since high school graduation about five years ago. He's busy scanning the ground. Frantic, his head pivots left and right. He makes his way down my aisle.

"Hey, Robert. How you been doing?"

Robert looks up and lets out a big exhale. "Hi Jacob." He smiles, but it quickly evaporates. He's not giving me eye contact and keeps looking around the immediate area. "Say, you didn't happen to see a twenty on the ground?"

I blink. The right thing would be to just give the twenty to him. Robert wasn't a bad guy in high school, but I don't know him that well. I know he still lives at home and his parents are loaded. They live in a huge house. I reach for my pocket, but stop.

"Uh, no."

"Shit. I don't have my debit card and that was all the money I had on me." Robert's basket has lettuce, ice cream and a frozen pizza.

"That's a bummer. Hope you find it."

Robert leaves without saying another word and continues searching for the missing twenty he'll never find.

It takes forever in checkout. The woman in front of me can't get her credit card to work. A manager has to come to override the till or something. Then her card gets declined. The people behind me begin to slip into other check-out lines. I would too, but I'm the very next person up after the woman who can't get her financial shit together.

Finally, after fifteen minutes, I step out of the grocery store. It's dark from the thick, heavy clouds. What the hell? It was supposed to be clear as a bell, nice and hot.

Now I'm running late. Maxine will be pissed if she comes over before I've cleaned anything. I don't know why she always freaks out so much. After all, it is *my* townhouse. She's got her own place. Maybe she thinks it reflects on her if my place is too messy.

I should text her to tell her I'm on the way. Before getting in the car I pull out my phone. My bag of groceries starts to slip off my fingers and when I go to adjust my hold of the bag, I lose grip of my phone. My eyes widen as I see my phone tumble down. The corner of it hits the asphalt and it comes to rest, right side down.

I hold my breath. Maybe my OtterBox case saved it. I turn the phone over. The entire screen is cracked. Grrr, there goes $900.

I fume all the way home. Why wasn't I more careful? I should have put the groceries on the ground before I took out my phone. Or I should have waited until I was sitting in the car.

It was Maxine's idea to host a barbeque. She invited a few of her friends. Jorden said he'd come as well. Me and Jorden used to be real tight even after high school but I haven't seen much of him since I started going out with Maxine a year ago.

I pull up to my place and park behind Maxine's car. So much for getting here before her. The first raindrop splatters on the windshield as I'm turning off my Hyundai. That's when I realize I forgot to text or call her. I was so pissed-off after I dropped my phone that I forgot.

The heavens open and I get soaked by the time I make it to my door.

"Hey, sorry, I got held up at the store. The lady in front of me in line had a problem with her card and it took forever."

Maxine marches in from the hallway, barefoot with blue jean cut-offs and a baggy light blue t-shirt. She's also wearing yellow rubber gloves and is holding the toilet bowl brush.

"Why didn't you clean the washroom? I told you three times yesterday. You could have done it this morning."

"I ... uh ... I was going to do it as soon as I got home so it would be nice and clean and perfect for when everyone got here." Actually, I played video games last night and never got around to it. Then I slept in this morning and forgot and didn't remember until I was on the way to the grocery store.

Maxine shakes her head. "Whatever." She storms back down the hall. As I'm putting away the soggy groceries I can hear her harping from the bathroom.

"You had all the time in the world and did *nothing*. Now I've got to take care of it. And you want us to live *together*? I'm not your maid."

I look outside the front window. It's totally pouring. The rain is almost to the level of the curb. I also notice that I left my driver's side window open. Great. I check the weather on my phone's cracked screen. It still says it's supposed to be hot and sunny. I frown. How wrong can the weather guy be?

Maxine comes into the kitchen and pulls off the yellow gloves and chucks them under the sink. "Why didn't you at least wash the dishes instead of just standing around?"

I shake my head, "Sorry ... I ... "

"Did you remember to get the vegan burgers for Coreen?"

I slap myself on the head.

Maxine crosses her arms. "Do I have to do *everything*?"

"Sorry." I smile and move in for a hug. Maxine lets me, but I can tell she's really annoyed. I rest my head between her shoulder and head. Her hair smells great. Maybe there'll be some action tonight after the barbeque?

Maxine's phone dings. We break apart and she reads the text. "Yvonne and Max cancelled."

"The way it's pouring, I don't know if we'll be able to have it. The street's totally flooded over."

Within the hour a few more cancel to the point where we call the barbeque off. Jorden is disappointed when I text him. Maxine complains about a headache and decides to go back to her place. Just as well when she's extra grumpy. She wasn't very sympathetic about my phone either.

The next few days are also crummy. On Sunday I forgot about the open window in my car *again* and someone rifled through it. Took all my change. Then I sat down and got a wet ass. I was twenty minutes late for work at the factory on Monday because my alarm didn't go off. My boss wrote me up. On the way home I got a flat tire. On Tuesday I cut myself peeling potatoes.

I know Maxine wasn't too happy with me on Saturday, but by Wednesday she still hadn't returned any of my texts or calls. What the heck?

I drive to her place on Thursday. She lives in an apartment closer to downtown. It's trendier than the suburbs where I live. At least my place is bigger and has closets. When it's time for us to live together, it makes sense that she moves in with me.

There's no answer on the first buzz. Her rusty Corolla is parked in her assigned space, so she has to be home. She needs to get a new car. I buzz a second time. Maybe she went for a walk. She sometimes does that. It makes me nervous because this part of town can be sketchy, especially at night.

"Hey, we're in apartment 312." It's a man's voice. Sounds like Jordan. I frown. Okay, that's weird. The door buzzes and I step in.

One of the elevators is out of service to someone moving. The other is on the twentieth floor. It's faster to take the stairs.

I knock on Maxine's door.

"Chinese is here," I hear just before the door opens. Yup, it's Jorden. He's only wearing shorts. His black hair is messy.

"Whoa." Jorden takes a step back and raises his hands. "What are you doing here?"

"What are *you* doing here?"

Jorden looks down and scratches the back of his head. "Um, the Chinese food guy was coming..."

Just then Maxine's land line rings the certain way when someone wants to get buzzed in. Maxine walks in from the hallway wearing a skimpy pink nightie. "Why didn't you buzz him in the first time?" she says but then screams when she sees me.

"What the ...?" I say.

"W-why are you here?" she asks. Her face is like a bright red pepper.

"Yeah, he asked me the same thing. You've ghosted me for four days and now I know why." I look to Jordan and clench my jaw. "You're supposed to be my best friend."

Jorden takes a few more steps back to stand beside Maxine. She throws on her housecoat that was draped on the couch.

The phone buzzes again. Maxine crosses her arms. "I'm sorry, Jacob. I ... we ... I've felt us drifting apart the past while..."

"Drifting apart? We were going to host a barbeque on Saturday! It's Thursday. You never talked to me since then."

"I know, I know. I should have told you earlier. After I left on Saturday I called Jorden to see if he could help me with the car. I needed a boost. He came over and..."

"...and you cheated on me." I shake my head. "And some friend you are," I say to Jorden." The phone buzzes again. "You better get that, you're food's getting cold." I turn and leave.

I readjust the towel on the seat of my car before sitting down. The heat's made the interior smell moldy and gross. I slam my hand on the dash. What the hell is going on? It's like everything is falling apart. I stare out the windshield at the street and take a deep breath. Just before I start my car I catch a glimpse of the twenty I picked up at the grocery store poking out of my pocket. I pull it out. Despite being rammed in my pocket, it still looks pristine. No folds or creases. I haven't worn these jeans since that Saturday, but still, that's kind of weird. I stick it back in my pocket,

On the way home I get into an accident. Nothing major. Just a fender bender. The guy in front of me stopped suddenly and didn't have any brake lights. Still, it will likely end up being my fault. I glance at the house we're in front of while exchanging particulars. Number 20. And the other driver happens to be twenty years old.

I frown. I was twenty minutes late for work on Monday. I haven't had a chance to get it yet, but my flat tire will cost $20 to fix. Why is everything twenty?

When I get home I grab a beer, fall into the comfy chair and turn on the TV. It's on channel 20. I take a sip of beer and pull the twenty out from my pocket again. Still in perfect condition. I fold it in half and run my thumb nail over the crease. I unfold it. Still no crease. I rummage through the utility drawer in the kitchen and find the scissors. I try to clip the corner of it but the scissors are useless. It's like the thing is made out of Kevlar or something.

I hold the twenty up. Everything's been going in the toilet ever since I found it on the ground.

I've got to get rid of it. I go over to the corner store and get a bottle of Coke from the cooler. I plop down the twenty. The girl behind the counter takes it and gives me my change. There, that bad karma is gone.

I check my messages before leaving the store. The guy behind me buys a pack of smokes with a fifty. The change must include the twenty I had. Good, that guy can worry about it.

Before leaving the parking lot I roll down the window in my car. Just as I slip the gear into DRIVE a piece of paper hits me in the face. Garbage flying around on a windy day. I look at it. It's the twenty.

What the hell? The guy must have dropped it. I look around. He's gone. How did it get out of his wallet? If it's the same bill, maybe he rammed it in his pocket and it fell out, like how Robert lost it at the grocery store.

I stop at a red light at a busy intersection. There's a homeless guy on the median trolling for money. He's got a small cardboard sign that says *SPARE ANY CHANGE. GOD BLESS!* I roll down my window and flash the green. He's about three cars away. The dude's eyes light up and he runs towards me. The guy steps awkwardly from the curb and twists his ankle. He falls in a heap. The light changes to green. I'm holding up traffic while the homeless guy is in pain. I drive by him and try to throw the twenty out of the window, but it blows back into my car and flutters in the back seat. Through my rear view mirror I can see it stuck to the back window, staring me down.

A letter in the mail from the landlord says that my rent is going up $20 a month.

I try burning the twenty, but the match burns down to my fingers. The twenty still looks perfect. There must be some kind of curse or hex on it. This is nuts! I feel like I'm in an old episode of *Twilight Zone*.

This was Robert's twenty. I lied and kept it. I should have fessed up and given it to him when he was looking around for it. It's not like I *really* need the twenty. I was being selfish in a finders-keepers kind of way.

What if I give it back to Robert? It will set things right and maybe lift this crazy curse.

Robert still lives with his parents. He's one of those *failure-to-launch* kind of guys. I heard he went to university, but dropped out half-way through the third year. He works seasonal jobs or whatever his dad can find for him. Maybe he does need the money?

I pull up on the driveway of his parents' place. Three storeys, a lot of house for three people. There's a pool in the back. I heard the basement has one of those fancy entertainment rooms where a screen comes down to watch movies like you're in a movie theatre. No wonder Robert doesn't want to move out.

Robert answers the door with a quizzical frown. "Hi Jacob," he says. We don't see each other for years, meet up at the grocery store and then I show up at the door. Of course it's going to be weird.

"Hey, uh, remember I saw you at the grocery store?"

"Yeah," he replies, tentatively. His eyes are searching me, looking for my angle.

I pull the twenty out of my pocket. "Anyway, I found that twenty you lost. Not sure when I'd see you again, so I figured I'd pop by to give it to you." I hold it out to him.

Robert tilts his head to the side. "I got my money back at the store. Some old lady approached me and said she found it. I don't know about the twenty you found. Maybe someone else lost money at the store. Thanks for thinking of me, but I'm good. You might as well keep it and consider yourself lucky."

What? It was that old crone. She's behind all this. Some kind of witch or something. Maybe she's getting me back for bumping into her or she's giving me bad karma because she knew I kept the twenty when I should have given it Robert? There's no way two people lost twenty dollar bills in the same store at the exact same time.

"No, you can have it." I thrust the twenty towards his hand. "It's not mine, so you might as well have it."

Robert moves his hand away and is frowning like he's creeped out. "Uh, no. I'm okay. I don't need it."

"You sure?"

"Yeah, anyway, I gotta go. See you later." Robert closes the door with me still holding the twenty.

In the days that follow I lose my job and get a parking ticket ($20 fine). Then there are the little things I attribute to the curse of the $20 bill including various trips, falls, dropping dishes, the TV breaking down and someone throwing a rock through my window. By the end of the week the transmission in my Hyundai craps out.

The walk to the grocery store is a long one. Along the way I get splashed when a driver zooms through a huge puddle. A snarling, loose dog bites my pant leg. A kid in a bike spits on me. A random nut job swears at me.

I hang around the tomatoes at the grocery store. After about ten minutes I spot the old lady carrying a basket with apples and carrots. She has the same scowl as before. I approach her while she's feeling the oranges.

I pull out the twenty and smile. "Excuse me."

She turns. A frown slowly forms on her lined face.

"I believe you dropped this." I hold out the twenty.

The crone squints. A faint smile crosses her lips. "Yes, I believe so." She accepts the bill. "You've learned your lesson."

I nod.

She turns and continues examining the oranges.

I spin around and leave the grocery store. It feels like a burden, a weight, has been lifted. A young woman going into the store smiles at me. A car stops so I can cross the parking lot. Near a bus stop I see a fifty dollar bill leaning against a sign pole. It looks like it's in perfect condition. No one ever finds a fifty on the street. I bend down to pick it up, but stop. I put my hands in my pockets and walk home.

Richard Zaric's historical fiction novel, Hiding Scars, was published in 2018. He is presently presently pitching his second book, a young adult novel called Stealing Amazing Fantasy #15. In 2020, Richard won the Two Sisters Publishing Romance Short Story Contest. He has had short stories published in anthologies including Through My Eyes in 2021 and Rabbit Hole V earlier this year. Another short story will appear in the Corporate Catharsis: The Work from Home Edition anthology later this month from Water Dragon Publishing.

Time Travel $5
Ed Teja

Harvey Alder settled back behind the wheel of his silver Tesla as it headed (on autopilot) up Highway 180, heading northwest out of Silver City, New Mexico.

Just outside the town, the landscape changed dramatically — mountains became hills and the vistas opened up, the vegetation became sparse, and the closest thing to a tree in sight was scrub that he heard the locals called New Mexico clumps.

The road was practically empty. To someone like Harvey, who came from a smaller state (and forty-five of the states are smaller), the area looked almost lonely.

"It's like going back in time," he told his wife Ruth, who sat beside him. "Just imagine the wagon trains crossing all that open land."

"It's pretty dull," she said with a hint of distaste. "But it looks like a place where they'd make one of those Western movies you like. Miles of miles."

He nodded. He couldn't expect her to like this place. She was a city girl and had come along to placate him. For his part, he'd promised they could go on a cruise later in the year. She'd probably already booked it.

Their vacations were like that. They seldom agreed on an "ideal" spot and divided up the time, part for her and part for him.

It was getting increasingly hard for Harvey to find a place he liked. When he took a break from working, he wanted quiet and laid back. He wanted a rustic area where he could sit with a beer and stare into space. Unfortunately, many of the places he had loved a few short years ago now sported all-inclusive resorts. Ruth was delighted.

From his perspective, the future looked bleak. At thirty-five, Ruth was already planning their retirement. Of course, they would live in a senior development of some kind. She wanted an apartment ("I'm not going to spend my golden years gardening," she said), that was near a golf course, and a place that offered regular activities.

It all made Harvey's head hurt. More to the point, it had him wondering about other options.

For instance, what would it be like to live quietly in that rundown adobe house he could see a little way down a dirt road? What about a frame house nestled among two or three others in one of these tiny little towns that were only on the map because there weren't any bigger towns within two hundred miles?

That was something he could see himself doing. He'd buy a comfortable rocking chair, stuff a cooler with beer, hire a Mexican cook/housecleaner and spend his days on a shaded front porch, living like a king.

The dream was pleasant, but only a dream. Already Ruth was bored. She would be angling to get back to New Jersey as soon as possible. And his job, designing telecom circuits, wasn't something he could do from here. Still…

"You don't like this area, do you?" he asked.

"Santa Fe was all right," she said. "It's more of a town than a real city, but it's nice — in a quiet way."

The way she said the word "quiet" spoke volumes.

"It is wonderfully quiet out here," he said.

She turned and gave him her hard stare. "Harvey Alder, don't tell me you like it way out here in the middle of nowhere."

He shrugged and decided to do as she asked. He wouldn't tell her. "You're right about it being just like the cowboy movies though. And this isn't just an area where they make them, many of the stories those movies are based on happened around here. The story the movie Stagecoach was based on ended in Lordsburg, just south of here."

"Well, all this open space is different," she said. That wasn't a compliment. "Fine enough for a visit, I suppose." Then she spoke under her breath. He didn't catch the words but didn't have to. "A short visit," would be the sense of whatever words she'd used.

He pointed at a building ahead, as he slowed for a drop in the speed limit that signaled a town ahead. "We can stretch our legs."

She peered through the windshield. "I see a little store up there." She pointed at a small, quite old, reddish-brown adobe building that sat back from the road.

"I see it," he said, slowing to pull into the unpaved parking lot. If she shopped, he'd get a chance to look around.

"Souvenirs," a hand-painted sign said.

"Maybe there will be something to get for gifts," Ruth said. She wasn't expecting much.

"I just want to stretch," Harvey said. Then another sign caught his attention.

"Cold beer and snacks.
Carlos' special homemade burritos.
Time Travel
Handmade moccasins
Gold nuggets"

"Now that's a funny assortment of things," she snorted.

"How do you think they sell it?" he asked.

"What?"

"It says they sell time travel." He grinned. "Think it comes by the slice?"

The joke earned him the usual blank look that greeted all his attempts at humor, anyone's attempt at humor. Robin Williams would have had trouble getting a chuckle out of her. "You can ask them what that means," she said.

"I would think you'd sell time travel by the year. Then, since it's under beer and burritos, I thought maybe they did it like pizza — time travel by the slice."

As usual, having to explain it ruined everything. He wondered why he bothered.

"Whatever," she said. I want to see if they've got any of those konchinka dolls."

"Kachina," he said. "Not konchinka."

"Whatever."

Going in the front door triggered the ringing of an old-fashioned bell hung over it. It clanged annoyingly, announcing their arrival in a musty store where they confronted an odd assortment of housewares that were probably hot sellers back in 1880. Harvey almost giggled at the array of kerosene lanterns, washboards, flat irons that were meant to sit on an open fire to get hot, and what would be a cornucopia of goodness for a movie company making westerns.

The small man who looked up at them, from fussing with something behind the counter, could have passed for a prospector from the same era. He lacked a bushy beard but had soft brown shoulder-length hair peppered with silver. He wore a work shirt, jeans, and a vest. Although Harvey couldn't see his feet, he felt it was a safe bet that the man wore cowboy boots — rough ones, not fancy rodeo boots.

"Help you folks?" he asked cheerfully. He came out from behind the counter. Sure enough, he wore battered boots. "Name's Chris Hopkins, and this is my store. If you see anything you like, let's dicker."

"I was looking for those —" she glanced at her husband, then said, "konchinka dolls."

"Well, we got us a few," the man said, grinning. "They aren't a big thing, locally, though. If you're looking for real high-quality ones, you'd do better to check out the ones they sell on the reservations."

"Reservations?" she asked.

"Yes, ma'am. The Indian tribes make 'em and they have stores on the reservations."

"Indians?"

"Apache, mostly around here. Navajo and Zuni and Hopi to the north. They've usually got a large selection of authentic ones."

She scowled. "Maybe another time." She stared at Harvey meaningfully. "I'm not sure we have time to visit a reservation. Why don't you show me what you have? It's just something to give our nieces."

Nodding, the man started toward a counter in the back, but Harvey pointed at a sign on the wall behind the counter that was similar to the one outside — the one listing items for sale. "What the hell does that mean?" he asked.

"Which one?" Harvey caught the twinkle in the man's eye. The store owner smelled a sale and now he'd jiggle the bait. That would be interesting.

"Time travel. Who sells time travel?"

"Just me, far as I know."

"But what does it mean? What do I get if I give you five dollars?"

"Why, it means you go on a trip. We can send you traveling back in time. Not sure I can add much to that, although I have to admit that with our setup, the adventure usually involves a little travel through space on top of that. Not far. Mostly you go through time."

"For five dollars?"

"What about the dolls?" Ruth asked.

The old man made a face. He pointed to the back. "They are right against that wall. If you want to check them out, all the dolls I got are on that shelf, Ma'am."

"Thank you," Ruth said, wandering back.

"You are telling me you sell trips through time?" Harvey asked.

"Five bucks," he said, nodding.

"For five dollars?"

"That's as low as I can go, I'm afraid."

"I don't understand. You expect me to believe you can send people through time?"

"Yes, sir." He looked flustered. "I don't mean I expect you to believe it. That's your call, but yes, for five bucks, I will send you through time."

"If you can do that, why is it so cheap? Or is this like Disney World, and you create a fake past?" He looked around. "I bet you just walk the customer through some kind of museum, right?"

He scowled. "No, sir. This is your genuine article. Time travel… the real thing. And the reason it don't cost any more than that is that it ain't all that popular."

"People believe it works, but don't want to travel through time."

He grinned. "Most don't want the full trip. Pretty much everyone around here took the sample run but then figured they was better off in the here and now they know. Every once in a while, we still get a few who want the real deal, though."

"Why wouldn't people want to go through time?"

He shrugged. "People got all excited about the idea when grandpa first got it, I understand. But then they take the sample run, and when they know it's real… well, they get thinking that the past isn't much like it is in the movies."

"What do you mean?

"People get romantic notions about the past. But when it comes to going… well, I remind them they can't get French fries when they want, or maybe even clean clothes… I mention that folks weren't so big on sanitation in the old days, that upsets folks some. When they realize where they'd be really heading, some people aren't so eager to go."

Harvey thought of Ruth and understood.

"What time period do you send your customers to?"

The store owner put his hands on his hips and grimaced. "Well now, I can't quite rightly answer that. I would if I could, but it seems to vary some with each person we send back. Mostly, I'm guessing folks go back to the old West — somewhere in the late 1800s."

"You are guessing?"

"Well…" he rubbed his chin. "It's not like the cartoons. You can't dial in a time."

"So you have no idea where you are sending people?"

"Well, I peek through just before I send folks back. It's a safety thing to make sure they won't step into the middle of a gunfight, or off a cliff. Like I said, there can be a location shift. From the clothes and buildings that I see, I think they pop into sometime around 1890. Silver mining boom times. I guess that's good. I wouldn't want to send someone back and have them in an ice age or get eaten by a dinosaur."

"I would think not. Bad for business." Harvey wondered what the scam could possibly be. The man seemed to be doing his best to discourage business.

"Of course, like I said, it's been a while since we used it."

"You haven't gone back?"

He laughed. "If I had gone back to 1890, I wouldn't be here. I would have died of old age by now."

"So people don't return after a fixed period of time, say, a year or two?"

He shook his head. "There's no machine at the other end. Far as I know, it's a one-way trip. I reckon that's part of why it ain't so popular."

"Can't you just open the portal or whatever and look back at that era?"

The man sighed. "Damn thing closes shut after a moment or two. Once it shuts down, I have to put it in the sun to recharge for a few days before it works again."

"Can I see the machine?"

"Ain't much to see," he said, pointing.

Harvey laughed. "That's your time machine?"

The man was pointing at an old-fashioned scale — the kind you put in a coin and find out what you weigh.

"Well, that's what we use."

Harvey laughed. "That's a scale. I don't want to weigh myself."

"It just used to be a scale. For a penny, it told your weight and fortune. The machine Grandpa bought is inside. It's just a little cube thing. Grandpa and the alien fixed up the scale to control and house the machine. The alien didn't want to give up his control panel in the trade, cause he needed them."

"Alien?"

"Some fella that wandered in from the desert. Said he was stranded and needed some things so he could make repairs to his vehicle. Turned out, Grandpa had everything he needed, but the alien didn't have any money. He did have a time machine and Grandpa bartered for it."

Harvey tried to picture it. "An alien crashed here and traded a time machine for parts from… this store? An alien?"

"Who else would come in here with a time travel machine to trade?" He made it sound commonplace.

Harvey smiled with relief. "Okay, you got me. You conned the city slickers. I almost fell for it." He looked around. "I'll take a couple of beers."

"It's not a con, sir," he said, sounding offended. He went to the machine and patted it on the coin slot. "This baby is the real deal."

"The scale that travels through time."

"Yessir. Well, that sends you through time."

"Always back in time?"

He chuckled. "Now you are trying to trick me. You know well as me you couldn't send a person to someplace that isn't yet."

Harvey pointed at the machine. "I'd think that if that really worked, you'd have a line of people outside this store willing to pay $5000, easy, to use it."

"That's sort of what Grandpa thought, too. That's why he made the trade. Good thing he wasn't out of pocket much for it. I imagine we've broken even by now, though, so we can't complain."

"I'm surprised that word of this never reached the government. If it works…"

The man laughed. "It did. Grandpa said they sent a fella out here during World War two. He came over from Alamos. Heard about it from some workers who passed through and taken the sample ride."

"And he didn't confiscate it?"

"He was thinking about it. He took the sample and then said he needed to test it proper and if it worked, the government would want it — for the war effort."

Harvey grinned. "And it failed."

"No sir. He insisted on going through. That was the last anyone ever saw of him. When some agents came looking for him, Grandpa told them what happened, and they didn't believe him. Just decided he was one of them whackos, I guess."

"And this machine can give me a sample trip?"

"It can send you back ten minutes, more or less. That still costs five bucks, but because it doesn't use up all the power, I can give you a sample ride and, if you like it, send you back for real the same day. If your wife wants to go, she'd have to wait a day while I recharge the machine, though."

Five bucks! That was nothing. "How does this sample work?"

Chris shrugged. "Just a low power run that only sends you back about ten minutes. Now, sometimes there is what they call spatial displacement as well as temporal." He grinned. "That means that after the sample, you might find yourself in another spot and have to walk a spell to get back here."

"And you can do that right now?"

"For five bucks, absolutely. That's what it's for."

"What if it doesn't work?"

"You get your money back."

"You aren't going to do that, are you?" Ruth asked. She emerged from the back holding several dolls. "You know you can't travel in time, no matter what this Mister Hopkins claims."

"Thinking about it," Harvey said.

"A simple waste of five dollars, if you ask me."

"No, Ma'am," Chris said, "if the machine doesn't work as advertised, then he gets his money back." He grinned. "I'll tell you what, if it don't work, I'll let you have one of those dolls for free. If it works, you buy all three for the marked price."

Harvey grinned. The man knew how to dicker. "That sounds more than fair enough," he said. "What do you think, Ruth?"

"Well —" she said.

"You want the dolls? How can you pass that up?" Harvey teased. He realized that he'd been worried he'd look foolish by trying. What other angle could this fellow have? But this way, making Harvey feel like an idiot would cost him money.

"All right," Ruth said. She gave Chris a suspicious glance. "So, I have to pick one of these dolls."

"I'll make it three dolls if you like," he said, sounding cheerful.

"If you are serious, I'm going to put them in the car now," she said. When Chris and Harvey both nodded, she headed for the shelf. "Buy me a beer and I'll be right back."

And so Harvey found himself committed to a test ride.

"The beers are on me," Chris said, going back behind the counter and grabbing three cans. He put two on the counter, opened the third, and came around to the machine, drinking his.

"I'll wait for mine until I get back," Harvey said.

"I'll put it back in the cooler while you are gone," Chris said with a wink.

Ruth came in and opened her beer. "Did you travel in time yet?"

"Not yet," he said.

"Just give me a fiver and hop on the platform and we can get 'er done," Chris said.

It was just plain silly, but Harvey had to admit that he trembled slightly once he'd handed Chris Hopkins five dollars and gotten on the scale. Nothing was going to happen, of course, it was just a bluff of some kind. Not that he had any idea what the point was. What did this Chris Hopkins get out of coning him?

"Check your watch," Chris said. "Compare it to my clock."

Harvey glanced at the clock on the wall and noted it was five minutes faster than his Tag-Heuer. An idea came to him. "So does your machine alter my watch? That doesn't count for time travel."

"No sir, it sure don't. I was just suggesting it as a reference point for you. Your watch should tell you the truth and when you come in, compare it with my clock."

"I'll be here watching to make sure there is no funny business, like him resetting the clock," Ruth said.

Chris touched his arm. "I suggest that when you come walking back to the store, if you happen to see yourself here, don't come charging in. Check your watch and don't come in here until after this time — it's the time you left, you see. Once, we let some folks meet themselves and it didn't go well."

"I could see that," Harvey said. He wasn't stupid, after all. Or was he? He was stepping onto the scale after paying some hillbilly five dollars because he said the machine would send him back in time. How stupid was that?

Chris slurped his beer, then leaned over and put a token in the slot of the scale. "The alien made these," he said. "Nothing else works. We got two types…one for the test and one for the full deal."

"What happens when they are gone?"

Chris grinned. "We reuse them."

As the scale swallowed the token with a soft metallic clink, the room spun around. Well, it wasn't exactly a room spinning, it was everything spinning. Ruth was spinning and Chris was spinning and blurring and fading into everything else… everything that was spinning and blurring and fading.

Then he found himself alone on a dusty patch of ground. The thought struck him that he should have brought a compass. Feeling slightly weak and dizzy, he scanned the area, looking for the road. He couldn't see it from where he was standing. But then, in the distance, he saw a building that had to be the store.

He looked at his watch. It said it was a little more than ten minutes before the time it had been when Chris dropped the token in the machine.

Impossible!

He took a breath. Whatever had happened (and he knew he'd sort it out. He was an engineer, after all) he needed to get out of the hot desert sun. With no other destination in sight, he took a deep breath and began the trudge toward the distant building.

After about five minutes, a car scooting along the horizon caught his eye. That had to be where the road was, just the other side of the building. The machine had sent him (teleported?) out into the boonies. As he walked, he saw the car pull into the parking lot.

The car looked familiar. It came to a stop and two people got out. He stopped still and tried to catch his breath as he watched Ruth and… he — himself. The couple was talking as they walked up to the building and went inside.

Harvey went to the car and took a close look, then touched it. It was his car. He had been driving it — it was now a few minutes before he'd gone back in time, the moment they'd arrived at the store. Another deep breath calmed him enough to edge closer to the door.

He could hear voices inside. Not words, just murmurs.

He glanced at his watch. Two more minutes. He fought the aching urge to barge in and see if what had happened before was what was happening now.

Finally, he cracked open the door. Himself, the other Harvey, stood on the scale glancing at his watch.

Chris slurped his beer, then leaned over and put a token in the slot of the scale. "The alien made these," he said. "Nothing else works."

A sudden hot breeze ripped the door from his hand, and it slammed open. Ruth turned and stared. "How did you do that? You were right here."

"I just got here," Harvey said.

"No. You've been here all along."

"He's just back again," Chris said. "You kinda have to try it to understand."

"No," she said. "Obviously, it didn't work. You may have created the illusion of sending him across the room, but that isn't time travel."

Harvey grabbed his beer from the counter and opened it, taking a big swig. "It's hot out there."

Chris agreed. "Even ten minutes is a long walk in the desert at this time of day."

"What are you going on about?" Ruth said.

"Time travel," Harvey said. His excitement built. He pointed a finger at Chris' chest. "If I go back in time, it's like that? I'm just there?"

"One extra step. You'll see a portal and you have to step through it. Like volunteering."

"And I can see what I'm walking into?"

"You see a time and place. I assume that's where you end up. I'm just guessing. The alien didn't leave a manual."

"And if it doesn't look right?"

"You don't have to go." He paused. "But no refunds if you change your mind at that point."

Harvey pulled out his wallet and found a five. "Let's do this." He knew he wasn't thinking clearly. The idea was crazy, but he had to explore this, find out what happened.

"Sure thing. I suggest you leave your wallet and watch and phone with your wife... anything that wouldn't be right back in that time, here."

That made sense, as much as anything about this made sense.

He emptied his pockets, putting everything on the counter, even coins, even his beloved watch.

"Harvey? What the hell are you doing?" Ruth asked, her question soft, concerned.

"Going back in time. It's the chance of a lifetime."

"What about me?"

He turned, eyes wide. "Do you want to go too? That would be great."

"No. I'm not doing that. I really wish you'd—"

But Harvey was already on the scale, his heart pounding. The old west, here I come. "Put in the token."

Chris slipped the shiny gold token in the slot and then stepped back to peek through the portal. What he saw looked like pictures he'd seen of the town of Pinos Altos back when the mines were really going strong. Well, it would be easy for his customer to find work, which was a good thing, since he had no money.

They never thought about that. Not once in the years he'd been doing this had anyone thought about how they'd pay for anything in the past.

Harvey stood frozen in place—the natural reaction. "Holy —" he said, but Chris didn't hear the rest because Harvey stepped forward and the portal closed behind him.

"He's gone," Ruth said.

"Just for a moment," Chris told her. "The universe has to readjust.

"What does that mean?"

He put up a finger. "Wait for it," he said, already feeling the ripple beginning to run through the fabric of the universe. Well, that's what he called it.

A glance at the counter reassured him that the man's things were gone.

The woman, now wearing a nice print dress and with her hair done differently, scowled at him. "Well, can you tell me how much I owe you for the dolls and the two beers?" she asked. "My husband is waiting in the Winnebago in your parking lot."

Chris looked at the pile on the counter. "Sorry, Ma'am. That's fifty-five ninety-eight."

She handed him three twenties. "Keep the change."

"Thank you."

She nodded at the scale. "Isn't that one of those old-timey scales that gives you a fortune with your weight?"

"Sure is."

"Is it for sale?"

"No. I'm afraid not."

She shrugged and took a card out of her purse. "If you change your mind, send me an email with a price."

He glanced at it. Ruth Preston, Boston, MA.

"Glad to, Mrs. Preston, but don't get your hopes up. I'm rather fond of it."

She pointed at the sign over the counter. "My husband was curious what that sign is all about. It says you sell time travel."

Chris wiped his face. "Just a joke, Mrs. Preston. Everything here is from the area and pretty dang old. My Grandpa told me sooner or later I'd be able to charge folks for coming in and visiting the past."

She chuckled. "That's a good one." Then she paused. "With the right marketing, you might be able to do exactly that... sell people a glimpse of the past and call it time travel."

"Now there is an idea," Chris said.

Then he walked her to the door and watched her get into the RV. As it pulled out, he decided to have another beer.

No, he'd open that bottle of whisky. It wasn't every day he managed to sell his quota of time travel. Heck, it had been months now since they'd had a customer. It was nice that the next time the alien stopped by to get his cut, Chris would have an interesting story to tell him.

He liked hearing the stories and might find the last of the parts he needed to fix his ship in that Tesla.

Ed Teja is a lifelong storyteller, as well as a former boat bum and magazine editor. His recent publications include short fiction in Ellipsis Zine, Millennial Pulp Literary Magazine, Frontier Tales, and Nova Fantasia. His crime story PARTY BOAT will lead off the new season of the mystery podcast Mysteries To Die For in 2023.

Creature Blindness
Cass Richards

For as long as I can remember, I have felt like an alien living among strange, confusing humans. Where some people go through a phase where they look at their family and wonder if they might have been adopted, I used to look around and daydream that I had been left on Earth by accident and had a cool name like Kal-El. It completely made sense to me then when, in my early twenties, I found out that I was neurodivergent. But if putting a label on what's going on in your brain can explain a lot, it doesn't necessarily make your life any easier. As much as I tried and as much as I wanted to, I was never unable to *quite* fit in anywhere. I wasn't unhappy, though. I had a job that I loved as an illustrator/concept artist (mostly digital). I had my cats, my books and my own fantasy world... until, of course, actual magical creatures started to pop up all over the world and turned my life upside down by making my art, and myself, irrelevant.

#

It's quite ironic that the thing that makes me special these days is also the thing that I hate: the fact that, unlike everybody else, I *don't* see magical creatures. That's right. I just don't... and I have yet to meet someone like me. In case you're curious, I can also tell you that I can't even *touch* them: try to put one of those scalding salamanders in my hands and not only will I not see it, it will go right through my hands. To you, though, it will seem as if I wasn't able to catch it. That's what confused me the most when it first happened: how I seemed to be living in a complete different reality.

It also sucked that the sudden apparition of magical creatures (something I had actually dreamed about for years), made me even more alienated from others: I had spent my life living in my own world of fantasy creatures, finding comfort in it, when, one day, this world became an   actual reality for everybody else but me. My inner world was still there, of course, but it had lost its coziness and had turned dull and flat, as if its very substance had escaped into the world.

At first, I thought my own neurodivergent perception of the world was to blame and I started to hate that complex brain of mine and how, because of it, being different had suddenly become another source of self-doubt and isolation. Until the Mythicization happened, however, I had never really seen being neurodivergent as a bad thing. Since I am also an incurable introvert and suffer from social anxiety, I quite enjoyed the melancholic solitude of feeling like an outsider. I liked being at home, sipping my specialty teas surrounded by flickering candles and the earthy smell of incense. I have a few friends, and family of course, but I didn't really understand how heavy loneliness could feel until everybody started to see wondrous things burst out of the woodworks of everyday life, and I didn't.

As a result, this "magical world" people suddenly found themselves in became a source of frustration and alienation for me: if a friend pointed to a fairy pollinating her wildflower garden or at an Earth gnome hiding behind a flower pot, I had to pretend that it was incredible and felt terrible for lying to them. When my sisters shared a picture of the rare thunderbird that went viral last month, I only saw blue skies and a few clouds and I secretly felt angry at them for showing it to me. Yes, the daily clips and photos people see every day online are, to me, pictures of empty streets, beaches and skies, which is kind of strange... but also sad because Heaven knows I *wish* that I could see a Kitsune or, as cliché as it is, merfolk... but I just can't.

When a few weeks passed and I was still blind to magic, I started to look for others like me. I posted a few things online under different profiles to see if I was the only one to experience "creature blindness", but nobody ever wrote back. All I got were hurtful messages from trolls (not the magical ones, unfortunately) and thoughtful messages from strangers, but nobody else seemed to be quite like me.

Then, one day, I started to think about the whole thing differently. I was sitting under my favorite maple tree in my grandmother's backyard, watching her as she was talking to a visiting jackalope when I suddenly realized how crazy she looked, bent forward like that and talking to a tuft of flowers. This is when it hit me: "maybe I can't see this jackalope because it doesn't exist." Think about it: why would *not* seeing magical creatures make me crazy? From my perspective everybody was sharing pictures of a whole lot of nothing.

So as time passed and as people's encounters became more and more frequent and diverse, like the Kappa that took residence in Toronto's High Park pond and the reports of a Mishibijiw in lake Biwa, near Kyoto, I started to doubt the reality of what was happening to everybody else... Until, of course, I finally saw something that, quite literally, changed everything.

It all happened about six months ago, when I was on a date with a girl named Cassandra. It was my first "in person" date in quite a while and my first with a woman since I had decided (without really telling anyone) that my pronouns were she/they. I was terrified to be out in the world again but also, quite paradoxically, relieved because I felt like myself for the first time in a while. My relationship with Cassie had started on social media before switching to text messages and, finally, to a couple of video chats where she didn't seem to mind my awkwardness. It may have been natural for her to meet someone soon after having met them online, but it wasn't for me. So despite my initial nervousness and numerous freak-out moments (where I almost cancelled our date) I appreciated the fact that Cassie had pushed me out of my comfort zone. So when she suggested we go for a walk in a wildlife park not far from her painting studio, I just said yes.

From what I had gathered online, the park was known for its lake, nestled within a dense birch grove, and had recently become popular because some people had seen a unicorn roaming among the trees. I wasn't surprised by that choice because, like many people I know, Cassie had a fascination for mermaids and unicorns (mermaids being, according to her, on the terrifying spectrum of awesome.

As we entered the cloister-like world of the grove on that crisp autumn morning, marveling at the delicate balance of Fall colors surrounding us, I initially managed to silence my insecurities. It was not an easy feat for me because a) I had never told Cassie about my "creature blindness" but also because b) she was way more intimidating in person, with luminous skin, rich brown hair and that special glow that contrasted with my short-haired, gangly self. As we walked side by side, I tried to act as normal as possible with my hands thrust deep in the pockets of my oversized jacket, hoping she would not notice the clicking sound of the magnetic stones I was using as stim toys. I really wanted to take her hand and get closer to her but I repeatedly glanced at her instead, keeping our conversations entirely imaginary and my hematite stones clicking.

After maybe twenty minutes of walking in what I perceived as an increasingly awkward silence, Cassie looked up, stretched and took a deep breath.

"I like nature so much, it's such an inspiration. Like recharging the creative batteries, don't you think?" she said.

I was staring at the wisps of mist that were coming out of her glossy pierced lips as she talked, lost in their intricacy.

"Lex?"

"Yeah! It's... pretty," I croaked as I suddenly realized she was talking to me.

She frowned at me, raised an eyebrow then chuckled.

"Come, the lake is nearby," she said as she nodded towards the trail.

I raised my fist. "Yup, let's do this!" I said, this time way too perkily.

The date was definitely going the way most of my previous dates had gone, and that was not a good thing.

The small lake at the end of the trail was, to me, the closest thing to a fantasy setting we had seen since we had entered the park. Its surface was perfectly still and mirror-like except for bright yellow leaves that drifted like flakes of sunlight on the dark obsidian water. Fog was unfurling from the golden birch woods surrounding it, giving it an even more ethereal dimension. As blind as I was to all things magical, the trees felt, for a brief moment, like the living pillars of a cathedral where every rustling was a whispered prayer. I honestly wouldn't have been surprised to see a hand come out of the lake, holding a sword.

"So? What do you think?" Cassie whispered.

"Wow it's like a medieval tapestry," I said.

"It's almost too perfect, right?"

"Yeah... I-"

Cassie suddenly inhaled and crouched, grabbing me by the arm as she got down.

"What are you doing?" I said.

"Shhh!" she said as she got on her knees, obviously not minding getting her pants muddy and wet.

"What?" I said as low as I could.

Cassie ignored me and, very carefully, looked from above a line of reed-like plants. She got down again, her hands in front of her mouth.

"Oh my God, I can't believe it," she said, her voice now barely a whisper.

I slowly moved from a crouch into a squat and looked at the lake which was now slightly tinged by sunlight. At first I didn't notice anything remarkable, except that the breeze was touching the surface of the lake, drawing fine wrinkles. Then I saw movement in the trees, followed by a red flash. I felt my heart skip a beat until I realized that what I was seeing was a pretty but totally ordinary cardinal.

"What was it?" I said as I crouched back down, trying to sound casual.

Cassie frowned and gave me a quick side glance.

"What do you mean? The u-ni-corn?" she said, tilting her head towards an empty line of trees.

I felt my heart drop and was surprised it didn't completely fall out of my chest.

"Oh, wow... so you were right about this place," I said, hearing my own blank disappointment.

She turned towards me, looking a bit confused and, since I was clearly looking in the wrong direction, she gently grabbed me by the elbow and forced me up.

"What are you doing? She's right there! Look before she's gone! Aw, she's so beautiful..." she said, her voice trailing in a child-like whisper.

I glanced distractedly at the edge of the forest, trying to imagine what a unicorn might actually look like in real life.

I heard Cassie sigh.

"No, come back! Oh, you're so pretty!" she then said, her cheeks flushed and a spark of tears in her eyes.

I stared at my companion, the only beautiful thing I could see in these woods, and started to feel envious of her intense reaction for what, to me, was a beautiful but unicorn-less forest.

"Yeah, she's really beautiful. I love her... horn," I managed to say not realizing that the creature had already left.

I had my last real in-person conversation with Cassie an hour and a half later, as we were walking towards my favorite coffee shop. I felt cold and depressed and the streets, perfectly mirroring my state of mind, were wet and plastered with crumpled brown leaves. The sky was still cloudy, with the sun casting occasional blades of silvery light that delicately touched my pale, freckled skin. I took a deep breath and tried to focus on the beauty of that day, hoping it would not end as badly as I feared now that Cassie knew about my condition.

"I'm so, so sorry Lex. I would never have suggested going into that park if I had known," Cassie said, not as physically close to me as I would've liked.

I shrugged and felt a shiver run through my body as a cold wind passed through the streets, shaking wet leaves loose from the trees above.

"It's okay. It's my fault. I should've told you but I just... didn't know how."

She bumped me gently with her elbow and I almost lost my balance.

"You can trust me, you know?" she said with a wink, getting a little bit closer. I managed to smile and look at her briefly in the eyes, feeling giddy despite myself.

"Thanks, Cass. I guess it's like when someone has hallucinations, you know? It's not something people talk about on a first, hum, date," I said.

Cassie came closer and put her arm in mine. I instantly felt my heart beat faster as a warm glow spread through my whole body, making my hands and neck tingle. For the first time since Cassie and I had physically met, I started to feel my body and mind relax.

"I understand. How does it feel, not to see what everybody else can see?"

I hesitated for a few seconds. Unsure of what to say.

"We don't have to talk about it, you know? I'm sorry I'm curious," she said.

"No, it's okay."

I tried to get closer to her without tripping on my own feet (something I had a habit of doing). I felt a bit dizzy by her physical closeness, yet safe enough to open up about myself.

"I don't know. I mean I've never seen any of it, you know? So I guess I don't know what I'm missing," I continued.

"But your art is all about fantasy worlds. Don't you wonder what it's like?"

"What, to be like everybody else? I do. Sometimes. But, I mean, if someone had told you, before all this, that they had seen a Qilin passing through their yard, what would you have said?"

"Nothing, I guess. I wouldn't have believed them."

"Yeah, exactly. It's just hard for me to believe what everybody else sees."

"But this is different, right?"

"What do you mean?"

"Well, *everybody* sees them."

I slightly disengaged my arm from hers, letting a bit of the cold from the outside creep between us. I always felt like retreating from people when I felt misunderstood by them.

"So, what, they must be real because *everybody* sees them? Your reality changed overnight and you all accepted it without ever questioning it. But it's not *my* reality," I said, a little loudly.

"But that's what reality is, right? What the majority agrees on?"

"I really don't know, Cass... I mean I can't even touch those creatures so, for me they simply don't exist. I might as well be standing next to you, but in a different universe," I said as I took a few steps back.

Cassandra walked towards me and took my hand in hers.

"It came out wrong. I mean it must be very lonely to see the world the way you do," she said, looking at me with a crooked smile. "I'm sorry, Lex."

"Please, don't feel sorry for me," I said as coldly as I could manage.

I felt my jaw tense up as I tried to push the bitterness away. I could tell that she was struggling to understand me and that she wanted to be nice to me but I also knew that she would never quite see the 6world the way I do. So for a fleeting moment I really felt like letting her go. I simply didn't want to feel alone in a relationship. But she came closer again and leaned her head on my shoulder, melting my resolve.

"I mean I'm sorry that we can't share the beauty of this world together," she said.

My mind went blank at the sudden intimacy and I turned towards her but ended up awkwardly kissing her hat, which smelled of roasted chestnuts and cinnamon. I was about to mumble an apology when I realized where we were.

"Ah, almost there," I said as we turned around a corner and entered the street where the coffee shop was located. I was starting to mentally practice my order of a pumpkin matcha latte with blueberry-peach crumble when my eyes caught sight of something large looming over the city.

"What the *fuck* is that?" I said, stopping in my tracks, feeling Cassie's head pop up.

Hovering high up above the highest buildings and partly hidden in the clouds was a huge, ominous-looking spaceship.

I was standing in the middle of the road, trying to get a better view of the structure that was spinning very slowly above the downtown core of the city. I call it a spaceship because it was the first thing that came to my mind when I saw it. The more I looked at it, though, the less certain I was about its nature, for it didn't seem like something that could travel through space or be able to fly anywhere. It looked like an old upside down city, or an accretion of buildings of various sizes, shapes and colors. From the distance I could see, at its base, square-shaped parts that looked mostly grey with a crumbly aspect to them. There were rectangular structures on top of the squares, dark and rusty. Jutting out from it all were huge spear-like projections that reflected the sun, clouds and sky like modern high-rises. The whole structure also emitted vapor like a city in winter.

"Lex, you're scaring me," Cassie said, bringing me back to my senses.

"What? You don't see it?" I said, unable to look away.

"See what? A magical creature?"

"No, a sp-"

I looked down and stopped myself, for it was clear that Cassie could not see what I was seeing. I looked around at the people passing us by in both directions. Nobody else but me was looking up.

"Nothing, I... thought I saw something in the clouds. Over there," I said pointing.

"What did it look like?" Cassie said, looking exactly where the flying city was and apparently not seeing anything.

"It was right there. I guess it was just a shadow in the clouds," I said, shrugging as I took out my phone.

I snapped a picture and lo and behold, there it was in my photograph. I zoomed in on the picture, noticing antennae-like objects, holes that could have been windows and a whole lot of very realistic details that made the whole thing look very real. I almost laughed at the incongruity of the situation. I took another picture of the flying anomaly, this time with the buildings under it and passed my phone to Cassie.

"It was right there. A big round thing. Like a... spaceship" I said tentatively.

Cassie looked at my phone then passed it back to me with a smile.

"It would have been cool, though, don't you think? First magical beings then *spaceships?*"

"Yeah," I said, wondering what the hell was going on.

From that moment on, I went down the Internet rabbit hole and ruined the rest of the date as I simultaneously tried to figure out what the hovering thing was while trying not to freak out in front of Cassie, who was eyeing me from above her coffee cup.

I typed "spaceship" in the search engines on my phone but the "news" section came back empty, typed "flying city" and other combinations of words but all I got were regular sci-fi themed webpages. I then tried to check webcams from around the world and felt my heart drop when I saw other structures hovering above them. Paris, New York, Tokyo... Just like in invasion movies, structures seemed to have appeared above the world's largest cities. Not all of them looked like the one above my city but they all looked like permutations of the same elements. I looked around at the people in the cafe, feeling the urge to yell "what the FUCK?" but all around me customers were placidly ordering pastries, chatting, checking their phones and sipping their drinks. Whatever was happening to me and whether that thing in the sky was real or imaginary, I seemed to be the only one capable of seeing it.

"You seem worried about something. Is everything alright?" Cassie suddenly said, her voice literally plucking me out of my own thoughts.

"Ah, yes. Sorry."

"Is it because of that thing you think you saw?"

The thing I "think" I saw?

"No. I was, hum, looking up stuff about that unicorn," I managed to say, unable to come up with anything more convincing.

"Okay... I could paint it for you if you want," she said tentatively.

"Hum, yeah, thanks," I said, feeling the urge to go out and check on the structure again.

I'm probably crazy... Filling the void of my existence with spaceship delusions, I thought, feeling more and more agitated.

After a while, Cassandra announced that it was late and that she had to go back to her workshop.

"Ah. Okay. Are you sure?" I said, not even looking up from my phone.

"Yes. It's getting dark and I'm tired. You also seem busy with something," she said.

I looked in the coffee shop window behind her, noticing that it was already night out and immediately wondered what the structure looked like in the dark.

"Sorry I... get like that sometimes, when I need to find information about something. I just can't stop," I said, finding it hard to put the phone down but doing it anyway.

Cassie looked as if she was about to cry but in that moment I didn't quite understand what it meant for us. All my thoughts were focused on that thing outside and the need to see it again, to understand it.

"Maybe next time we can talk about it?" she said as she got up and put her jacket on.

I got up, put on my own jacket and looked around the table and chairs to make sure I hadn't forgotten anything, noticing that my cup was still half full.

"You know, I really hope we get to do this again," Cassie said with something that sounded like hope in her voice.

"Of course," I replied maybe too lightly. "Do you want me to walk you back to your workshop?"

"No. It's fine," she said, putting her large headphones on.

I stopped buttoning up my jacket, feeling somewhat guilty and wondered if I had said something I shouldn't have.

"Okay, I-"

She then nodded with a little awkward smile and was out the door before I could say anything more.

For more than six months I didn't hear from Cassie. I didn't blame her, though, for I was too busy with my obsession. I also knew that she had had her share of abusive and dismissive partners and that she deserved someone who truly cared about her. Not someone like me, obsessed with something that might not even exist.

The "spaceship" I had first seen remained above the city for about a week and then suddenly vanished. It was replaced by another about a day later, which also disappeared after five days in a kind of vapor-like blur, with bursts of twisted light around its edges like those you see around pictures of black holes. I have observed the structures both with the naked eye and through a telescope, and as much as I have captured them in photo or in drawing, I am still unsure of their nature. I have no idea where they come from or why they're here but I quickly understood that there are people on them because I could occasionally see things happening on the structures. For example, I saw bright reflections moving on their surface when the sun was shining at a certain angle, like windows opening and closing. I made time-lapse videos and marveled at the way the lights on the structures twinkled at night, as if there were people turning them on and off. I also saw lights that moved from one place to another, sometimes even between the buildings themselves. So, yeah, until I actually saw some of "them" on the streets I saw many things that could be something... or simply nothing, for the structures were always too high for me to see them clearly. I saw planes fly through them, making me feel crazy, but I also crashed an expensive drone into it and saw the debris fall to the ground, surprising people.

At first I thought I was crazy, of course... Then I started to think that I was the only person on Earth able to see something that nobody else could, something more real than fairies or dragons... Seriously, though, what is scientifically more likely to happen? Spaceships appearing on Earth? Or the sudden and inexplicable appearance of griffins and sea serpents? Don't aliens make more sense than magical creatures?

I say "aliens" but just like their "spaceships", these beings could be anything. I can tell that they are weirdly humanoid but also something else. They seem to be wandering in busy streets as a group, but I have also seen some of them wandering empty streets alone. I can't really tell you what they look like either, because it's a bit like catching something from the corner of your eye when you're alone at home. You see a shadow or a blur, feel a flash of dread before realizing that it was just your imagination and that you are, in fact, alone. Maybe these beings are just like the phasmids that can hide from other insects but not from humans... maybe these beings can hide from regular people but not completely from me. I have also been wondering about the appearance of magical creatures and if "they" might somehow be responsible for them but, of course, I have no way of knowing. All I know is that Humanity has been much less interested in the stars lately. After all, if magic and the sense of wonder are now officially here on Earth, why bother looking for them elsewhere?

After a while I decided that these beings were "Shadow People", visitors from another dimension, which made sense since every scientist says that distances in the universe make space travel impossible. I guess that since they were going to be a part of my existence I needed them to sound plausible... Whatever they actually are, though, in the end I decided to use them: I drew and painted their spaceships and what they might look like themselves and actually made money from these designs; the money I couldn't make with fantasy art. I even published two poems and three short stories in science-fiction magazines, which is ironic, really, for the genre had never been my kind of thing. And by that I mean that, to me, it didn't feel as cozy as fantasy. A few weeks after my last publication, Cassie sent me an email to congratulate me, and we started chatting again. I am proud of myself because until now I have been able to *not* mention the Shadow People to her, which is quite a feat since it's the only thing I wanted to talk about until now.

In the end, though, I got used to seeing the spaceships appear and disappear above the city, got used to seeing and ignoring the shadows on the streets. Even though they never acknowledged me, they somehow helped me feel less alone. I must admit I also quite like being the only one to see them and know they exist. I have even started to write a novel about my experience. It's about a person like me, who is the only one on Earth to see that the world has become a sort of alien zoo, an all-inclusive collection of Earth's real and imaginary creatures to an amazed but unsuspecting humanity. Whatever the truth might be, writing this story is helping me makes sense of it. At least a little.

Looking at my life, today I guess that nothing has really changed for me: people are still in a world different from my own and I am still locked outside of it. The only difference is that instead of staying inside and drawing fantasy worlds, I am now outside a lot more, looking up, thinking about what's out there. I have even enrolled in a Graduate program in astrobiology. I may be an artist at heart but, who knows, maybe one day I'll be able figure out what's going on and do something about it... Maybe I'll also find out that I suffer from "creature blindness" for a reason, and that my special brain and I were meant to save the world... What a nice fantasy ending for my somewhat sci-fi life story that would be.

How I Met My Sirenian Wife
Brandon Case

It wasn't love at first sight, for she has many branching arms, like a fern.

It wasn't love at first touch, for her skin is moist, like a fern covered in milk.

It wasn't love born of conversation, for I cannot speak the language of ferns.

But her scent! Sweet ambrosia! She wafts lavender wine, and strawberry mead: a cocktail of pheromone bliss that forever intoxicated my heart.

The Captain warned me not to remove my helmet on Sirene—that I'd return from shore leave married to a repulsive alien.

I can only conclude he has an awful sense of smell.

My Favorite Alien
Ryan Marie Ketterer

I miss the smell of stale cigarettes and low tide. That's what Newry used to smell like, even if you weren't near the coast. Now, the smell of rotting corpses overtakes everything.

The rubber soles of the girl's worn sneakers crunch on the overgrown gravel as she scurries up behind me. I don't look over my shoulder. I need to move faster.

"Pa, why can't we go home?" she says. "Maybe Ma is waiting for us."

Home. Even though I know the danger, I slow down, stop. My throat aches and a bubble rises from my chest. Several long seconds go by before I can continue walking.

She fiddles with a few rocks, and then adds them to the small bag she carries. I don't know why.

I forage a few cups of berries and some green stuff I know wouldn't be poisonous from the limited forests surrounding the coastal town of Newry. Spear a rabbit, too. Boy Scout knowledge finally coming in handy.

Approaching the shelter, I scan the horizon for any movement. Sometimes my paranoia feels pointless. An overgrown parking lot surrounds me. Everything is still. Silent.

The building stands tall. I'd already scavenged all five floors of apartments. Blankets. Food. Carried it all down below.

I didn't want the high ground. I wanted to be below, hidden from the outside. The basement is protected, secure. It has small windows, up near the ceiling, that I use to keep an eye on the perimeter.

I step through the front door of the building and head down the long hallway. I hold my breath as I pass the first-floor apartments; homes turned into coffins.

"Close your nose, move your toes." Her nasally voice comes from behind me. The smell can be overpowering, even knock a person out if you're not careful.

Once inside the basement, I shut the door and nail a large piece of particleboard to the frame. It probably won't help much, if anyone ever discovers this hovel, but it's all I have.

I flick on the single bulb. The yellow glow brightens the girl's blonde hair. Just like Talia's.

"Pa, I'm hungry..."

I ignore her complaints.

In the early days, I was lucky to find a functioning generator. It sits outside one of the basement windows, the long extension cord running down the wall to the freezer. Until now, abandoned cars have provided enough fuel.

I can only hope no one hears it.

Before long, I expect it will give out.

The girl slinks to her corner. She dumps the rocks onto the concrete and murmurs something under her breath.

Three years before

The girl digs at the sand faster and faster, launching it over her shoulder.

"Gretchen! Stop throwing that, you'll hit someone," I say.

Our five-year old stops her furious task and grins at us. "Sorry, Pa!"

She continues digging, this time in a more controlled manner, and Talia smiles from across our small—but mighty—beach spot.

"Reading anything good?" she asks.

I show her the cover of my book, another astronaut biography I had picked up at the Newry Public Library.

"I shouldn't be surprised." She laughs, grabs her water from the cooler, and adjusts her chair to the sitting position.

I put my book down and watch Gretchen shaping the damp sand. I want to crawl over, to help her, but I know she'll shoo me away, insistent on doing it herself. It was only last summer when I first taught her how to wet the sand and shape it into anything she wanted. Every year feels shorter and shorter as she continues to grow.

"Look, Pa! It's gonna be a spaceship, just like the ones you make!"

My heart flutters as I give Gretchen a small smile, but when I glance at Talia, I notice the corners of her mouth are turned down, ever so slightly.

I've done my best in recent months to curb the talk of rocket ships and space travel. With space tourism on the horizon, Talia and I always loved to plan our pretend—but entirely possible—future vacations with Gretchen. What we might be able to do if we could visit the Moon, or maybe even Mars.

Gretchen loved it. But in the aftermath of Talia's stroke, space travel is all but ruled out, at least not without some sort of technological advancement that could reduce the effects of microgravity on the brain.

Traveling to space wouldn't have been the same without her, so I have resigned myself to remain here on Earth, with Talia.

Now

The rabbit meat is lean, tough. I chew endlessly before swallowing the masticated muscle.

The girl won't look at me.

I think I will go to the roof tonight. I hope the clouds from earlier will have burned off enough to see the stars. To see what could have been.

I walk up the six flights of stairs quickly, my eyes having long ago adjusted to the darkness. Nighttime is the only safe time on the roof.

I lay down on a quilt, taken months ago from one of the empty apartments below, and relax.

"The clouds are gone." Her voice sounds like sunshine.

I point at the sky. "There it is. Big Dipper."

She raises her hand, next to mine.

"I wish I could touch it." Her fingers flex as she tries to grab the stars in her hands.

"The stars you can see now are already gone. Their light just takes so long to reach us here on Earth." I don't know why I'm explaining this.

She lowers her hand. "But that means there are new ones out there, right? Ones we can't see yet."

She's a smart girl.

She pulls out one of the rocks she gathered earlier and rubs it between her fingers.

"I wish we could build a spaceship and go towards the new stars. Maybe there are aliens out there."

Clouds come into view and I wipe my eyes.

Two years before

"I love you," Laurie says as she pulls off her *Starsight Engineering* polo.

I smile at her in the mirror while taking off my own clothes.

"I can't believe those Norwegian execs. Their list of must-haves?" She has strong opinions about the direction of the new space cruiseliner we're building. "This isn't the ocean. Don't they understand outer space has completely different physics?"

"I don't have much time, Talia wants me home for dinner. No more work talk."

"Isn't all this work talk why you love me so much, though?"

She's not wrong. Talia's request to not discuss space or rocket ships or anything of the sort has made being at home a nightmare. But Laurie understands. Laurie is one of my best engineers.

"I know, I know. But save it for tomorrow. Right now I only want you."

Laurie sighs and lays back on the bed. I crawl in next to her, and pull her into my arms. She still smells like the manufacturing floor. Her eyes are a radiant blue and every time I look at her I get lost, falling too fast into her gravity well to pull away.

We kiss for only seconds before my phone begins to buzz. I try to continue the intimacy, but she pushes back.

"You going to answer that?" she asks.

"It's probably just Carl. It can wait. No more work talk."

The phone stops vibrating, and I lean in for another kiss.

Buzz… Buzz…

She pushes me away again.

"Trent! Answer the damn thing!"

I turn over and grab my phone and see Talia's name lighting up the screen. I answer.

"Hey hun, I'm finishing up at—"

"You were supposed to pick up Gretchen at school. You promised me you were going to take care of this today."

Fuck.

"I… Work's just been so—"

"Save it, Trent. Just come home."

The line clicks.

Laurie is silent while I get dressed and gather my things. My shame is like a block of cement in my gut. I kiss the top of her head and leave the apartment.

Traffic on the freeway is a knot at rush hour. When I finally escape down my exit, the sun is starting to set. I navigate the winding roads of Newry before rolling into our driveway. I head to the front door, bracing myself for impact.

But when I step inside, everything is quiet.

I walk upstairs, to our bedroom. Empty.

I drop my briefcase and take off my jacket.

Downstairs, the kitchen is still. The toys aren't strewn like normal; they're put away in the big chest in the living room.

I walk to the back door and look outside.

Talia is sitting on the deck, Gretchen wrapped in her arms. Talia's lips move: she is reading a story, the story she always reads, the story I used to read.

My Favorite Alien.

When I slide open the door, Talia pauses, looks at me, and then continues.

Gretchen doesn't even notice I'm there. It's like she knows. Like she can see the guilt in my eyes.

Later that night, I lay in bed with a book while Talia brushes her wet, blonde hair. Her brown eyes stare at me, empty, as she lists off my offenses.

"You didn't come home last night. You forgot to pick up our daughter today."

"Talia, I told you—"

"The excuses are bullshit," she says. "I'm sick of it." She kicks something. One of my shoes. It flies across the room and dents the eggshell wall.

Now

I ration out some thawed jerky from the freezer. It's held a taste for about a year now. The girl sits on a folded up blanket on the floor, under the only bulb, reading her book again. She reads the words out loud:

The blue alien is from the planet Stronia. Blue aliens love the ocean. They are dockworkers and fishermen.

The pink alien is from the planet Agolok. Pink aliens are engineers and scientists. They like crunching numbers and performing experiments.

The green alien is from the planet Jantara. Green aliens like to paint, sing, and dance.

Who is your favorite alien?

I'm stitching together furs from previous hunts and trying my best to leave her be.

Her voice stops narrating the silly story. The pause lingers.

"Why isn't Ma here with us?" The question comes up every day. I'm not sure why. I wish it would stop.

I bite into my piece of jerky. "She's with us every day."

Her face is confused as she chews her own meat. I step away. I can't help her.

Darkness slowly leaks into our little enclave. Night is falling. Each minute feels like ten. Or a hundred.

Finally, I climb the stairs. A new, nightly ritual. The girl talks, her earlier confusion dissipated.

"The pink alien was my favorite before, but now I think the green alien is my favorite."

I don't reply.

"I would probably get on good with the blue aliens though. I love the ocean. I'm good at math though. Do you think I sing good?"

Just one more flight.

The metal door to the roof creaks and we lay in our usual spot, looking skyward. Another cloudless night. Sometimes the apocalypse can be beautiful.

Her hand reaches out and points. "I think that's Stronia."

She continues pointing. "And that is Agolok. And that is Jantara."

I look at the stars, the ones that don't exist anymore, and let the tears roll down my face.

"Maybe one day we can build a spaceship and visit all of them! Pa, you can still build spaceships right? I wonder if the aliens ever visit each other. I hope they do. Maybe one day they will visit us."

One year before

"...interstate is jam...unable to find...*bzzt*...grocery stores are alrea..."

I flick off the radio.

"This is crazy. It happened so fast." Laurie squirms in the passenger's seat and taps her fingers on the door handle.

"Almost there, don't worry." I drive slowly towards the gated launch facility, navigating around people in the middle of the street. "Soon enough, we'll be off this god-forsaken planet."

We were lucky we finished the cruiseliner in time.

A man slams his fist on my window and I hear his muffled voice through the glass. "You! Bring us with you!"

I pull the car past him and try not to make eye contact.

I think about Gretchen. She is with Talia. She'll be okay. Right?

We pull up to the booth and a security guard stops our car. He's flanked by men with assault rifles, ready to fire at anyone trying to sneak in.

"Step out of the car, sir. We'll need to do a quick inspection, they're being real strict today."

Laurie and I get out of the car. I hope the simmering crowd doesn't come any closer.

"Trent! Trent!" The voice carries over the shouting people. Talia, with a weary seven year old tossed over her shoulder, breaks through the mob and approaches the security booth.

"Trent. Please, you can't leave us here. You can't leave us behind." Talia is shouting. There is desperation in her voice.

"I'm sorry, Talia. You'll die on that ship. They won't take the risk, you know that."

"I don't care anymore. I need to try, I need to save us!"

"Let me take Gretchen, let me bring her," I say, as I reach for my daughter. I hadn't felt her embrace in months.

Talia twists away, keeping Gretchen as far from me as possible.

"I won't leave her with you, we both need to come. I don't care if I die on that ship. Just don't let us die here."

The horde is growing more raucous. My heart slams in my chest.

I step carefully towards Talia, hands raised. "Let's talk, let's figure this out."

She rubs Gretchen's back. The girl continues to sleep. I reach for my daughter.

"Please, Talia..."

With a sudden, vicious movement, I dig my fingers into Gretchen's dark blue shirt—her favorite, the one with a spaceship on the front—and pull. I need to save my daughter.

Both Talia and I have a grip of her shirt, and Talia screams, holding on to Gretchen for dear life. "You can't take her away from me!"

One of the security guards approaches, his gun inching up ever so slightly.

"Ma'am, please step back immediately."

Talia wrenches Gretchen from me, and the girl is now awake. She cries, confused.

"Why is Pa grabbing me? What's happening?"

Talia lowers the girl to the ground. "Stay behind me, okay honey?"

Before Gretchen can move, the guard puts his body in front of Talia and pushes her back. "I said to step back, now!"

Gretchen's discordant wails barely overtake the throng of people that has begun to surge towards the gates. She stands between us, looking first at me, who beckons her, and then at Talia, who continues to get shoved by security closer to the swarm that has somehow grown even larger.

My daughter spins away from me and runs to her mother, screaming, arms flailing. Talia shoves away the guard and grabs Gretchen. The guard raises his gun, and yells, "Back now. Everybody get back!"

Talia is part of the crowd now. A man to her left steps in front of her, protective.

"Why you pointin' that at a kid? Put that shit down, we're all just tryin' to survive!"

The man continues to march towards the guard.

The staccato beat of rapid gunfire pierces my eardrums. I turn to grab Laurie and see that she's been pulled away by another guard, past the gates. The crowd surges forward, collapsing in around me. The gate closes.

"Trent!" I can only hear Laurie now, in the distance.

The gunfire continues but only angers the crowd more. On my knees now, I crawl through stumbling legs, trying to escape. How would I get to the launch pad, to the spaceship?

I escape the stomping feet and turn to see the crowd trying to climb the high, barbed-wire fence. Bullets riddle their bodies before they make it far.

But there, left alone in the shadow of the mob, are the bloodied bodies of Talia and Gretchen. They are twisted, stepped on, and motionless. I run to them. I am useless. I sob into the bloody spaceship on my daughter's t-shirt.

Now

Sleep evades me.

I look down into the freezer at the piles of frozen jerky. I take a few pieces and put them on a table to thaw. Breakfast.

I wrap a blanket over my shoulders. The cold is coming. I need a plan.

I look at the girl. Her eyelids dance like eyelids do when someone is dreaming.

I think back to before. The gunshots. The surge of the crowd.

Nightmares finally embrace me.

When I wake up, the girl is gone. I panic. Scream for her. When I see the stars through the small window, I know where she's gone.

I clamber up the stairs, not yet fully awake. Shove open the metal door. There she is. Her rocks are spread out where I usually lie down.

"Pa, look!" She gestures towards the rocks, as if they should mean something.

"Dumb girl! Never come up here without me. Someone might see you!"

She doesn't react to my words. She never does.

I drop to my knees, no longer able to carry this burden.

Why is she here? Why does she haunt me?

Tears soak my face and I feel her standing next me. "Look, Pa. Tonight, we can see Stronia, and Agolok, and Jantara." Her small hands are pointing skyward. "I was keeping it a secret until tonight, Pa. But I finally found enough pieces."

I shake my head, unable to speak.

She continues. "I've been collecting pieces of alien ships. I find them all over. I brought them all up here, see?"

She grabs some of them and brings them back to me. "I figure once we have enough, you could build us a spaceship. Just like the ones you built before. Then we could go to Agolok and you can be an engineer again."

I don't know when I carried all these pieces of rock to the roof. I don't know if they're even really here. Just like the girl. I know she's not real. Can't be real.

I slouch against the edge of the roof and look up. I was so close to the stars.

If only Talia and Gretchen hadn't come to the launch site, I would be with Laurie now. I would finally be in space.

The tears continue, but the ghost of my daughter won't stop talking. She hands me a rock. I take it.

"Maybe if you build a spaceship and we go to Agolok, maybe Ma will be there. Maybe all of us can be happy again. Like before."

The words are too much. I can no longer bear the weight. I turn away from her. I wish she would leave me alone.

Her arms wrap around me from behind. They tighten in a childish hug. I don't understand how this is possible.

"Don't worry, Pa. You're still my favorite alien."

Ryan Marie Ketterer is from Malden, Massachusetts. Her work can be found in Dark Matter Magazine and CHM (both forthcoming), as well as several anthologies. She's a fan of the weird and uncanny, and her writing draws most of its influence from the works of Shirley Jackson and Thomas Ligotti. When she isn't writing stories, Ryan is writing code for a software startup in Boston, MA or training for another road race. You can find her on Twitter and Instagram at @RyanMarie47.

The Rarest of Species
Diane Dooley

I didn't see the girl—the one I'd been warned to stay away from—until the third evening. I twitched back the curtain from the window that looked out across the Atlantic Ocean, nothing between me and America except for the hunched figure, bare feet in the icy water, the wild island wind whipping her long, dark hair. "Best stay away fae the wild one, if ye ken whit's good fur ye." I'd barely been able to decipher the man's thick accent, and it had been the only thing he'd said as he'd driven me to this abandoned village on a desolate island, far, far from the nearest coast of Scotland.

"Wild one?" I'd understood that much.

"The girl," he'd said, dumping my luggage and equipment and supplies on the doorstep to the one-roomed white cottage that was to be my home for the next weeks of hatching season. "Just count yer wee eggs and yer wee baby birds and away back tae America," his tone leaving no doubt as to his opinion on my research study and my presence on this island. "Endangered species, my arse," had been his last words before getting in his rusted jeep and driving away, back to the sad, grey village on the other side of the island.

I'd expected the village to be quaint, the people friendly, the island magnificent. I'd been right only about the last one. But there was a jagged edge to the island's beauty. The wind cut through you, the rain icy and sharp as diamonds, the clouds looming and constantly threatening. My research notebook was empty. I'd found not a burrow, not a nest, not an egg, not a hatchling. Some scientist, I was. The girl turned and I let the curtain fall. Too late. She was staring, and soon walking, in my direction. I glanced at my front door, wondering if I should lock it, the man's warning still ringing in my ears. Maybe she was mentally ill? Perhaps she was even more hostile than the villagers? I laughed softly and shook myself. I must be about twice her size. And I was lonely. Three days of bad weather and seabirds as my only company and the time ahead stretching out like a prison sentence. I opened the front door and waited for her.

She was a tiny thing, wearing a plain white dress and wrapped in a dark woolen shawl. She stared up at me, curious and frowning.

"Hi, I'm Alex Goldman. I'm a graduate student researching —"

"Any tea?"

"Tea? No, um, sorry. I have coffee?"

She made a face, but then she nodded. "Invite me in?"

"Sure." I stepped back and ushered her into my cottage. "Sorry, it's kind of a mess. Still unpacking and getting organized." She swept in, her eyes hungrily snooping over all my stuff, ignoring me as she peered into totes and prodded into boxes. "I'm here to count —"

"What about that coffee, then?" She glanced over at me and waited until I was busy with lighting my little gas stove and digging out cups before resuming her examination of my belongings. I observed her. Huge dark eyes, long black hair, sharp features, very thin, and with the palest skin I had ever seen. Not beautiful. Not even pretty. Strange, sharp. More weird than wild, I thought. She reached into a box and picked up a brown packet with her long, talon-like nails. She stared at it, then looked at me inquiringly.

"MRE," I said. She just stared. "Dehydrated food."

"Food?" She ripped out a corner of the packet and sniffed it. She dropped it back in the box with a look of disgust.

I figured she wouldn't like my instant coffee much better, but I handed her a cup anyway. "No sugar, sorry. I have dried milk, though, if you want some."

"Dried *milk*?" she said incredulously. She stood with the cup of coffee in her hands, sniffing it.

She hadn't said too much, but her accent seemed different from the villagers. Softer, less guttural, more melodic. "What's your name?"

"Rhona Shear, my mother named me." She blew on her coffee and took a sip.

"Shear? Really? How strange. I'm here looking for a colony of shearwaters. An unusual sub-species has been reported as nesting on this island, but I've been unable to find them."

She carefully spat the coffee back into the cup and handed it to me. "Tea is better."

I set the cup down and reached into a box, pulling out a large, glossy photo. "Have you seen this bird?"

She glanced at it, then resumed poking through my stuff, picking up an old green thermal shirt I'd tossed onto my bed. "Big mountain," she said, waving an arm behind her.

The mountain that divided the island in two, with the village on the other side? "No. You see, *these* birds nest on cliffs —"

"Big mountain," she said again, stroking my shirt gently, before sniffing it. "For me?" She looked up at me, her dark eyes expectant. "Present please?"

"Ah, well, sure, I guess. But it's not clean. Let me..." She had dropped her shawl and whipped her dress over her head. Before I could even process how completely naked she was, she pulled the thermal shirt on. It was ridiculously large on her, the bottom hem touching her knees, the sleeves completely enveloping her arms and hands.

"Soft." She smiled. "Warm." She looked up me, her face completely different. Small, sharp white teeth, dimples in both cheeks, eyes shining.

Maybe she *is* beautiful, I thought, watching as she stroked the fabric, her hands eager and happy. "I'm glad you like it," I said, unable to keep the smile from my face. She reached out a hand and touched my cheek, running her nails through the three-day growth.

"Kind man. Good smile." Before I could reply, she scooped up her clothing and walked to the door. She pointed to the headland to the right. "When the sun touches food will be ready." She kept walking, back towards the beach, pulling off the shirt as she did so. I watched as she dropped her clothing on the remains of a small boat before walking into the sea. Soon she was splashing in the ice-cold water, her hair wet and slick down her back to her narrow buttocks, her small breasts dripping sea spray. I watched, entranced. She was absolutely weird and definitely wild. I should probably keep my distance. But she knew where I could find my shearwaters. And I believe she had just invited me to dinner. I watched until she left, noting she went into the last cottage in the row of eight, the only one except mine that still had a roof. And soon I could smell the sweet scent of peat smoke, and from her chimney a curl of it seemed to beckon me.

Her cottage had no windows and the door was cut in two with the bottom half closed and the top half open. I stuck my head in. "Rhona?" She was crouched in front of a large fireplace where the peat burned red, stirring an enormous black pot.

"Come in and be at rest, Alex Goldman," she said without turning.

I entered and looked around. On the back wall of the only room another half door was open, with a small red cow resting its head on the bottom section of the door, chewing cud contentedly. As my eyes adjusted to the dim interior, I noticed a pile of skins and blankets in one corner, more a nest than a bed. In another corner, shelving went up to the low ceiling, and was packed with a variety of containers, plates and utensils, and a large collection of knives. The walls were covered with a variety of things: fishing nets, the jawbone of a large aquatic animal, bird feathers, shells of all shapes and sizes, a large machete. A small amount of clothing was hung on hooks in another corner. There were no chairs or a table. Instead, a large piece of driftwood was set in front of the fire, where Rhona was now ladling soup into wooden bowls. "Smells delicious," I said.

"Sit. Eat."

I sat crossed-legged on one side of the driftwood and took the bowl and spoon she offered me. Suddenly I noticed the fourth corner of the cottage. A huge flat rock rose halfway up the wall. A candle burned next to a small packet of rice, a jar of honey, and what looked like a hand-knitted pair of mittens. "Is that a…a…shrine?"

She glanced at it. "The place the people put my presents." She lifted her bowl to her mouth and took a large gulp of the soup.

I stared down at my bowl. Chunks of fish and what appeared to be seaweed floated in the broth. I put down my spoon and copied her, taking a smaller sip in case it was disgusting. It wasn't. I closed my eyes in bliss. Sweet and salty, hot and nourishing. It was the best thing I had ever tasted. "Delicious," I murmured, noticing for the first time she was wearing my shirt. I took another, larger sip. "The people who give you presents," I said. "The villagers?"

She nodded. "Other side of big mountain they live. Bring me presents so I do not kill them."

I almost dropped my bowl. "K-k-kill them?"

She smiled and gave a little shrug of her shoulders. "Wicked people. Stupid people."

"I thought you said they bring you presents?" Things were becoming clearer. She didn't *seem* insane, but she must be. And the villagers, out of the kindness of their hearts, brought her food to ensure her survival. Except they hadn't seemed kind. Quite the opposite. I remembered the brusque words and sly glances, the hostile eyes and muttered insults. A small child had told me to go fuck myself. An old lady had called me a Yankee cockwomble, which I was certain was not a compliment. But that didn't mean they deserved to be murdered. I sighed impatiently, deciding to humor her. "So how many have you killed?"

"None. Yet. But if they break the covenant, they know their fate."

She was relaxed, smiling in the flickering firelight, her hands darting as she spoke, as if what she was saying was all perfectly normal. The good news was she *hadn't* killed anyone. No doubt it had just been an idle threat after an insult from one of those asshole villagers. I examined her from the top of her head downwards. She was too slight to kill anything. I'd seen her entire body. Bone and sinew and pale, pale flesh. Her arms were languidly long and when my eyes reached her feet, with their hard curling toenails I saw that each of her toes were joined by a gossamer webbing. I jerked my mind back to our conversation. "And what is this covenant?"

She reached to the side of the fireplace and brought out a clear bottle of amber liquid. She set it on the driftwood and pushed it towards me. "The covenant is the rules by which I and they have agreed to live by."

I picked up the bottle, twisting it back and forth, trying to read its faded, peeling label. It was very old. And had never been opened. I raised my eyes to hers. "Has anyone ever broken the rules?"

She tilted her head and smiled. "Not yet." She took the bottle and broke the seal, then fetched two earthenware cups from where they had been warming besides the fire. I thought I had her figured out. She must have lived in the village once and had probably been shunned, or even bullied, for the strangeness of her ways and her body. Webbed feet? Didn't some cultures regard that as a sign of the devil? Or something to do with witchcraft? Certainly, back in that dilapidated village the only building not in need of a thorough overhaul had been the squat, grey church. I could well believe that they were a God-fearing, superstitious lot. They'd made her life hell until she'd finally threatened to do something drastic. And so she lived out here on the edge of the world, kept warm and fed—as long as she never came back to the village. Poor thing, condemned to such a lonely existence. But what of... "Any family?"

She rose and took a small jug from the shelf, ladling water into it from a crock by the alter-like rock, before returning and kneeling in front of the driftwood that divided us. "I had a family once." She took the bottle and poured. "My father's whisky in my grandmother's cups." She lifted the jug and added to the whisky. "Water from my mother's spring." She set the jug down. "On the driftwood that saved my grandfather's life." She looked up at him. "My family is never far away, though." She pushed a cup into my hand. "Drink."

The fumes from the whiskey, smoky and salty, made me almost dizzy, and I stopped with the cup to my lips. She couldn't be trying to get me drunk, could she? As a prelude to a seduction? She must be so very lonely. Maybe this desolate life had made her strange or maybe she had always been this way. I laughed inwardly. It would take more than a glass of good whiskey for her to worm her way into…whatever it was she might want of me. I had a perfectly nice girlfriend back in Maine, and with exactly no plans to go back to her with a guilty secret.

"Drink," she said again, almost pleading.

I took a sip. It was so wondrous my eyes closed. I took another, breathing out a huge sigh as I swallowed. She was staring at me, her cup shaking slightly in her hand. She lifted it to her mouth and downed the drink in one. I did the same. She set the cup down on the driftwood and stood up, breathing heavily. She stretched out her hand to me. "Time for bed, my husband."

"Stay away fae the wild one." The old man's words suddenly reverberated in my brain. I had seriously underestimated her level of crazy.

"Come," she said, beckoning with a flutter of her talon nails.

"I don't think…" I said unsteadily, mentally remembering the location of the machete and the knife collection.

"Silly husband," she said, effortlessly tugging me to my feet.

I didn't seem to be able to struggle, but my mouth still worked. "I'm *not* your husband."

She wrapped a sinuous arm around my waist and led me to her pile of blankets. She pushed me down gently. She was smiling. "You invited me into your home and I accepted. I invited you into my home and you accepted. You fed me. I fed you." She straddled me and guided one of my hands to her breast. "We partook of the Mother and the Father in the presence of the Ancestors. You are Mine. I am Yours."

I lifted an arm to push her away, but instead my hand caressed her cheek. Had she drugged me? I tried to gather myself, but her hand on my brow soothed me. "Silly husband," she said. "I will never, ever hurt you." And I knew it to be true. She never would. Ever.

Her first kiss was a peck. Literally. A quick bump of hard lips.

Her second kiss was only slighter slower, allowing her to dart a quick tongue into my mouth and back out again.

Her third kiss lasted the rest of the night, her eyes reflecting the glowing embers, our hands and bodies relentless and insatiable. All through the night we loved until, at last, the sun began to rise and we fell asleep in the gathering dawn, our bodies enwrapped so tightly as to be one, the entrancing taste of her in my mouth, and I in hers.

I awoke to a steaming mug of tea and Rhona's hair still wet from her morning oceanic ablutions. She wriggled like a warm fish in my arms as she fed me a plate of oatcakes, dripping with cream and honey. "Hungry husband," she giggled, stuffing the last sweet morsel into my mouth.

I shook my head wearily as I chewed and swallowed. "Look, Rhona. Don't get too used to having me around. I have my research to finish, and then I'll have to get back to the States. I know you've been lonely, but—"

"No," she said, cutting me off. "I haven't been lonely. I've just been alone." She rose and gathered up my clothing, tossing them to me, as she climbed back into her white dress and dark shawl. "Slow husband," she said, grinning. "You want to see your eggs and hatchlings now?"

I threw my clothes on in a hurry and followed her out the back door of her cottage. "I need to grab a notebook," I said, still shrugging into my woolen sweater. She didn't wait. Just started up the steep slope. "They're cliff dwellers," I yelled, rushing into my cottage and grabbing my notebook. I had to run to catch up with her. "You're going the wrong way!"

"Stupid husband," she muttered, and picked up her pace, over hummocks, through valley, around a small lake, and uphill, until we came to a jagged rent in the mountain, Rhona's black shawl flapping like wings in the mountain breeze. "Here," she finally said as we rounded a bend. "My ancestral home."

I stood, breathless, gaping, heart pounding, staring at the ruins of an ancient castle. I followed her into an old courtyard, with the remains of a crumbling fountain covered with moss. The massive doors no longer stood in the soaring entranceway. No roof, but the walls still towered around us. And on every perch, every stone, every outcropping, every ruined balcony were masses of birds — *my* birds, shearwaters — thousands of black eyes blinking and staring, as Rhona made her way through a maze of nests and burrows to a gigantic fireplace, still dark with soot. Everywhere were gleaming eggs and crying hatchlings. Thousands of adult birds. This colony was the biggest ever seen of this rare sub-species. I cursed myself for not bringing my cell phone. I could have recorded this! No one had ever seen a colony of this size, *this* successful. And in such a spectacular setting. I would have to come back. I needed to start counting. I

fumbled for my pen, and opened my notebook.

In the fireplace, Rhona spread her arms, her shawl dripping down over her white dress, matching the colors and markings of the birds. "You prosper, my cousins!" she shrieked.

One bird replied with a shriek of its own, then another joined in. As all the birds added their voices, the hideous cacophony of howling and screaming invaded my brain, and I was forced to cover my ears before falling to the ground in pain. The noise threatened to burst my eardrums as it changed from the sound of an army of ferocious dogs to the dying screams of women in childbirth. Everything became black and red. I must have passed out. Because the next I knew, Rhona had my arm and was hurrying me down the path away from the castle, away from the brain-bursting cacophony. I tried to pull away, to sit down, and gather myself.

"We must hurry," she whispered urgently, urging me on. "The villagers will have heard."

I looked around. It was growing dark. "How long were we in there?"

"Long enough," she replied, as she shearwaters dived and flew, following us, silent at last.

I stumbled and almost fell, but again Rhona caught me and pulled me onwards. "They will be coming to kill us," she said. "We must get back to my cottage before them."

"The birds?" I gasped.

"The villagers," she replied.

My lungs were burning, my legs trembling as we finally got back to the cottage. The narrow road that led over the mountain was bright with the glaring headlights of vehicles, and soon the first one squealed to a halt and disgorged its occupants: three men, carrying guns and tire irons. We retreated to the beach. They followed.

"You have broken the covenant," one man yelled, and I tried to run, to pull Rhonda into the cottage where we could at least lock ourselves in. More people were leaving their vehicles. A well-armed, angry mob was forming; men and women, adults and children, each carrying a weapon, their eyes lit with rage and hatred.

But Rhona would retreat no more. Instead, she laughed. "You *made* me break the covenant. You brought him here knowing I wouldn't be able to resist." She stroked my arm gently.

"Me?" I said. "*They* didn't bring me here. I came of my own free will; they had nothing to do with it."

She smiled. "Silly husband. Hair the color of the sun, eyes the color of the sky. Beautiful husband. They picked well. They brought you here so they would have reason to kill me."

"But..." The mob was advancing, slowly, waiting for the first person to take the lead, to break into a run. They crept forward on the lonely sand, weapons raised, teeth bared. "I don't understand," I said helplessly, trying to pull away. But Rhona held me firm.

"My family was here on this island long before these people arrived. We were generous. We gave them half, but nothing is ever enough for them." She raised her arms and tipped back her head. "I am the last of my kind. They wish to end me. I will not allow it." She dropped her arms just as the first villager raised a pitchfork to strike her.

A large shearwing swooped and dived, impaling itself on the prongs of the pitchfork. Then another. Soon, hundreds, then thousands, attacked the villagers, swarming them, knocking them to the ground with sheer force of numbers. The ringing in my head resolved into the sound of humanity screaming. A small child was having its eyes pecked out amid a flurry of black wings. An old lady groaned as bloody beaks pulled out her steaming entrails. The man with the pitchfork lay in front of us, eyes bulging, as a bird pecked and burrowed into his mouth, feasting on the stump of his tongue.

Everywhere I looked: blood. Every sound I heard: agony. "Stop," I said. "Make this stop."

"Gentle husband," Rhona whispered. "I will be merciful as you request." She clapped her hands and the massacre stopped. The birds flew away, en masse, a black cloud of furied flapping and dark silence, heading out to sea. Someone was crying. I think it was me. A few villagers were still groaning; a handful staggered back to their cars. The sound of engines turning over had never sounded so desperate, and soon those villagers that had survived were careening back over the mountain road, leaving their dead behind them.

Rhona took me by the arm and lead me through the bodies, though blood soaking the sand, back to my cottage. She put me to bed, and sat down beside me. "My father was a fisherman lost when he rowed ashore on this beach and met my mother. My grandfather was a sailor washed up during a terrible storm, clutching the driftwood that saved him." She stroked my brow. "They had the choice to leave and so do you." She leaned forward and kissed me gently on the lips. "But you should know I'll be laying a clutch of eggs soon. And I think you should stay to meet your children." She left me then, to a long night of nightmares and tossing and feverish awakenings, dreams of gleaming white eggs, the stretch of entrails and eyes and tongues, and Rhona's sinuous, vibrating body above me and in me and around me. And then oblivion.

I awoke at dawn, dressed, and put on my hiking boots for the long walk over the mountain. I'd decided to steal a boat from the harbor in the village, and somehow get back to the mainland and sanity.

Rhona was already up, naked in the waves, cavorting in the rising sun. Her arms were outspread like wings, and as she ran through the shallows, every now and then she would tilt, laughing, to the side, dipping her splayed fingers onto the surface of the ocean. The spraying droplets caught the sun, tossing shattered light all around her lithe and swooping body.

What *was* she, exactly? I sighed. She was the last of her kind, the rarest of species. And I was a scientist, after all. How many eggs would she lay? How long would they incubate? What would the hatchlings— my children, *our* children— look like?

The tide had come in and out again overnight, washing the sand clean, taking the bodies into the deep. It was like it had never happened. *Had* it really happened? Another peal of raucous laughter came to me on the wind as I ignored the abandoned vehicles on the road. I knew she would never hurt; would always love me. I was her husband, the father of her children.

And I was just a scientist, after all. I grabbed my notebook, and sat cross-legged in the open doorway of my cottage: May 15th, 2022, Day 4: I have discovered the rarest of species…

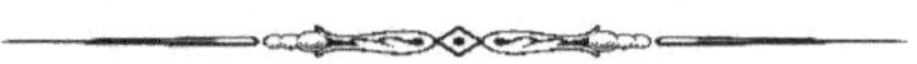

Diane Dooley's short stories have been published in The Literary Hatchet, Underground Voices, Liquid Imagination, *and more. Her novellas have been published by Carina Press, Kensington Publishing, and others. She can be found on* Facebook, Twitter, *and her* blog.

Graveyard Shift
Gideon P. Smith

The quiet of Alpha-Centauri hospice at night was electric. Soft sighs of infusion pumps and morphine-fueled dreams. Patients' auras danced like Earth's Aurora Borealis.

But when an aura faltered, I knew the end was near. Then, I would 'help'. I pared away their soul's tenuous grip, harvesting their failing energy for myself. Payment for this thankless job.

I was collecting bedpans when I spied Ms. Janey flicker. She lay trembling, blue eyes watery and afraid.

"Warm blanket?" I offered, approaching, ready to 'help'.

"No," she croaked, grasping my hand, And then she ripped out my life-force to re-fuel her own.

Only room for Just a few quick thoughts this issue on some of the many, many slices of fine SFF gracing screens large and small. First up, there's a new series of *Foundation* currently streaming on Apple TV+, and like the last one, it's sumptuous, expensively shot and somewhat baffling. Asimov's classic source text is a piece of pure 50's sci-fi, with a premise that worked then but makes zero sense now – what if you could use a giant planet-sized computer to *predict the future?* Well it might work if you completely change the storyline and just shoehorn in a few of the more colourful characters. Pity it all takes itself way too seriously. The clone emperors are fun though (but you don't need a Hari Seldon prediction to work out what's going to happen to them),

There's a new season of *Sweet Tooth* on Netflix, too, but I have to say the considerable charm of the first series is beginning to wear mighty thin. Following a disease-led apocalypse which kills most people, kids are being born more animal than human and are being treated less than humanely, killed for science and generally kicked around. Gus is a bright kid with antlers –and maybe all the answers .Maybe all will be revealed in the third and final series – though I'm not convinced this series will hold my interest that long.

Other comics related shenanigans continue to dominate: the much hyped *Flash* has finally come and gone with a massive fan backlash (presumably a combination of Ezra Miller's casting and the new DCU reboot making this film seem pointless). It bombed at the box office, which serves Warners/DC right of cancelling Batgirl, but it's actually not a bad film, with the welcome sight of Michael Keaton back in the batsuit .It's all multiversy , as is the current trend, but that leads to some interesting what-ifs, and it moves at pace - the time just flashes past (sorry).

Elsewhere in comics-land, Marvel's *Secret Invasion* finally made it onto Disney+, and although I don't think many people expected much, it still came as a bit of a disappointment, largely because (I guess) the star names you might expect in an adaptation of a comics series which was all about star names being taken over by skrulls were largely missing (unless you count James 'War Machine' Rhodes without his not quite A-list flying suit, which I don't). I guess they couldn't afford Robert Downey Jr, et all, though by all accounts this six issue series' eye-watering costs might have been better spent on a decent movie. Basic plot is that shape shifting skrulls try to take over the world because Nick Fury reneged on a promise (or just didn't get round to honouring it). Then the most bad tempered of the bad guys, Gravik, gets hold of some power-stealing tech to become a super-skrull, and things look bleak. Can Fury save the day? Actually one of the big problems here is that someone else saves the day, in improbable fashion, raising more questions than answers. Despite some reservations I enjoyed it but I can see why fans were miffed a the whole exercise came across as slightly half-hearted. Fury deserves more.

I've generally enjoyed most of Marvel's latest TV offerings , but they've been drawing an increasingly critical response, not least from Disney's new/old head Bob Iger, who thinks there's too much product diluting the brand. I'm not sure about that and I'd prefer to see more, not less, but they need to believe in what they're doing – and I'm not sure, right now, that they do. Next up are *Echo* on TV and *The Marvels* at the cinema, after which we'll   get a clearer picture on the future direction of the MCU. Blip, crisis or a load of fuss about nothing? Maybe *Daredevil*, coming in the spring, will save the day.

Star Trek: Strange New Worlds is currently streaming on Paramount and it's fulfilling all of its promise. Best Trek since the original Trek in my opinion. Definitely the best of the revival series (those the last season of *Picard* was undoubtedly brilliant). If not Star Trek how it used to be then Star Trek as it should be. Best SF currently on TV.

Sorry we missed loads of good movies and TV this time around – unfortunately a comprehensive   run-through   would squeeze all the stories out, and that would never do. But please let us know if you want us to cover one of your favourites if we   keep   ignoring   it   (we're   waiting, *Witcher* fans…)

There should be more *Doctor Who* to talk about next issue, with David Tennant back in the Tardis and newly landing on Disney +. Back to the future? I love time travel.

Mark Bilsborough

Deeplight

Frances Hardinge

Young Adult, or YA, fiction gets a bad press sometimes. We older folk sniffily dismiss it as something for the kids, at least we do if we haven't read any of it. Twilight (derivative), Hunger Games (derivative and badly written), Maze Runner (predictable. And zombies) etc etc. None of that's true, of course. Twilight is well structured and (assuming you can get your head round vampire romance) a pacy, satisfying read. Hunger Games is inventive and adventurous and anyone who says Suzanne Collins can't write has probably never read her. And while Maze Runner could have done without the zombies there's no doubting it has strong characters, a driving plot and some excellent worldbuilding. I blame Harry Potter (which is also better than (some) people give it credit for).

Which brings me to Frances Hardinge. If you're a teenage haunter of school libraries she'll probably be very familiar but to the rest of us, she's a hidden jem. She writes YA – characterised by teenage protagonists and a (relatively) straightforward narrative approach – but she writes it really well. *Deeplight* is hugely enjoyable. It's a fantasy novel set in some mediaeval-tech level world where the monsters are real. In the recent past, giant sea creatures are revered as gods and keep a chain of islands safe from raiders from the continental mainland. Or that's the fond remembrance now these monsters have all perished in a great cataclysm. Some people want to bring the monsters back. Which would be a very bad thing.

The story is on one level a coming of age tale where the young Hark and his manipulative friend Jelt scam their way into trouble, leaving Hark indentured to Lady Vyne and forced to look after a bunch of brain addled former priests in their dotage. The priests, though, know the true secrets of the god/monsters and Hark needs to prize them loose from the dying priest Quest. His friend, Jelt, is intent in getting him into more trouble but only succeeds in enmeshing himself with a monster's heart and slowly turning monstrous himself. If Hark can't unravel the mysteries of the deep and stop the monsters from returning, many will die. But he can't destroy the monster's heart without betraying, and possibly destroying, his best friend.

Harks loyalty to Jelt powers much of this story and it's a toxic relationship. Jelt just won't let go, and plays on Hark's trust and loyalty. Will Hark break free of Jelt's malign influence?

I enjoyed it, but more importantly so did a bunch of teenagers I tried it out on. I'm intrigued and entertained enough to seek out the follow up and other works by the same author. Frances Hardinge. Check her out.

Mark Bilsborough

Bad Cree

Jessica Johns

In *Bad Cree* Mackenzie experiences frequent nightmares in which she sees her dead sister, Sabrina, get eaten alive by crows. Mackenzie did not attend Sabrina's funeral because she moved out of her family's home in Alberta after the death of her grandmother, which created an atmosphere of grief that she found unbearable. Her nightmares are therefore rooted in guilt: not just of missing Sabrina's funeral, but of abandoning her family when they might have needed her emotional support. Still, they remain in touch with her. Aunt Doreen, whom Mackenzie confides in, invites her to return home so their family can put their heads together and think of a solution to her nightmares. Mackenzie agrees, deciding that the severity of her nightmares outweighs the awkwardness of reuniting with her family. Together, they find a way to defeat the wheetigo, a shapeshifting monster that terrorises not only Mackenzie, but the rest of Alberta.

What I like most about "Bad Cree" is its sleight-of-hand. When Mackenzie's nightmares persist even after reuniting with her family, she does research on the Internet and learns that most dreams occur during REM sleep. This motivates her to set an alarm that goes off every hour in the night, forcibly denying her nightmares by removing the REM phase from her sleep. Her solution, backed by "the science behind dreams", seems logical and effective, especially when she successfully staves off her nightmares for several days — so many days, in fact, that they "start to feel familiar". Only after she collapses suddenly in a bar do we realise how impractical her approach is. Of course she isn't getting enough rest. And yet, didn't we believe for a moment that she had conquered her nightmares? A more discerning reader might have spotted her collapse, but it struck me as both surprising and plausible. I was reminded of Chris Priestley's short story, "The Un-Door", which employs a similar sleight-of-hand. Maud, a con artist organising fake seances, screams for help in front of her victims before dismissing her outburst as the result of alcohol, when it is actually the ghost of her partner speaking through her. Like in "Bad Cree", the revelation feels unexpected and reasonable at the same time.

The rising action, however, feels slightly less satisfying. Mackenzie, her sister, and her cousin propose facing the wheetigo without their parents, based on a "gut feeling" that they have to vanquish the wheetigo by themselves. I find this explanation a little weak, especially since Mackenzie has just learned the value of seeking help from her family instead of keeping her problems to herself. I also find it strange that despite the parents' knowledge of the wheetigo's viciousness, they do not give a second thought to the vagueness of their children's explanation, much less insist on accompanying them. This is particularly ironic because the novel contains lengthy descriptions of the parents visiting their relatives to gather knowledge about the wheetigo, suggesting a climax in which the whole of Mackenzie's family battles the wheetigo together. Yet, the actual confrontation only involves Mackenzie and her two partners. This makes me wonder what the point of the visits was.

Still, I was hooked by Jessica Johns' conversational writing style, which created a cosiness that complemented the themes of family, trust, and female solidarity. "Bad Cree" is a light-hearted and comforting read that will appeal to anyone new to the horror genre.

Ryan Tan

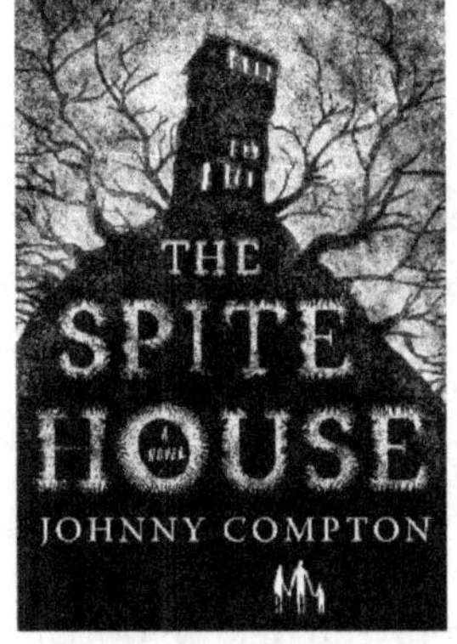

The Spite House

Johnny Compton

In "The Spite House", Eric and his two daughters, Dess and Stacy, are on the run. We only learn why towards the end of the novel: Stacy returned from the dead after being killed by a brain-eating amoeba, so Eric must hide her from their friends and family, who might report him to the police in the belief that he had kidnapped a child identical to Stacy in appearance. After eight months of driving from place to place and earning what he can, Eric needs money. This compels him to accept an offer to live in the Spite House with his family. All he has to do is journal his experiences in this supposedly haunted house, and his employer, Eunice, will pay him a six-digit sum of money.

I was most unnerved by the floating hallway of the Spite House. It "floats" because it is a recent addition to the third floor, putting it at risk of collapse. When Eunice's employee, Dana, gives Eric a tour of the house, she describes seeing "a lean, largely featureless shape" at the end of the hallway, reassuring herself, "Even if it were there — which it wasn't — it was insubstantial. As imposing and tangible as a memory." The juxtaposition of "insubstantial" and "tangible", and of the shape being there and not there, creates a sense of instability, like two enemies who are brought into close contact with each other, and who may lash out at any time. This volatility reflects the precariousness of the hallway, which may likewise collapse without warning. I also find it interesting that the words "lean" and "largely" are next to each other, suggesting that the shape Dana sees is, paradoxically, thin and bulky at the same time. It should not be possible for the shape to exist, just as it should not be possible for the hallway, and the house, to exist.

Given how three-dimensional the characters were, I would have liked the relationship between Eunice and her nemesis, Millie, to be a little more developed. According to Millie, she was once close friends with Eunice, who shared drinks with her, showed up at ceremonies where she received awards for her writing, and exchanged letters with her for nearly forty years. However, they became enemies after Millie published an article exposing Eunice's abuse of power in her hometown. I personally love the trope of former friends turning on each other because there is so much potential for horror in the cruelty and unforgiveness of human nature. Stephen King's "The Outsider" terrified me because I was appalled at the viciousness of the characters; having been friends in the past, they knew each other's weak spots and showed no mercy now. I didn't derive the same perverse satisfaction in "The Spite House", likely because Eunice and Millie's troubled history didn't feel central to the story. Perhaps their transition from intimate friends to cold rivals could also have been a bit smoother.

Nonetheless, the excellent dialogue injected the characters with authentic, compelling personalities. "The Spite House" is a strong debut and I look forward to reading more by Johnny Compton.

Ryan Tan

Don't Fear the Reaper
Stephen Graham Jones

Stephen Graham Jones delivers a head-spinning mystery, thrilling action, and gleefully over-the-top kills in *Don't Fear the Reaper,* his hotly-anticipated sequel to 2021's *My Heart is a Chainsaw.*

A postmodern tribute to slasher movies, *My Heart is a Chainsaw* introduced the lakeside town of Proofrock, whose bloody history – witch hunts, a fanatical cult, and a summer camp massacre, among others – has evolved into myth. Its unlikely heroine was Jade Daniels, a horror-obsessed Blackfeet teen who was the first to suspect a new killer at work.

Chainsaw, of course, ended with countless Proofrock residents butchered on Independence Day, during the town's annual screening of *Jaws. Don't Fear the Reaper* picks up four years later. Jade is back in town, acquitted of the lake murders but on parole for destruction of property, of all things. (Jade never could catch a break).

Fortuitously, Jade's arrival has coincided with the escape of Dark Mill South, a hulking hook-handed serial killer who might as well be played by Kane Hodder. The bodies immediately start piling up, the slayings referencing everything from *Silent Night Deadly Night* to *Happy Death Day* (which Jade hasn't heard of, since she was in prison when it came out). But Dark Mill South isn't the only one in Proofrock with an axe to grind.

Don't Fear the Reaper demands and rewards close attention. Jones narrates in a colloquial, stream-of-consciousness style, rife with internal monologue, digressions, misapprehensions, and seemingly throwaway details that turn out to be pivotal plot points.

Reaper is warmer and more leisurely than its predecessor. When we first met Jade in *My Heart is a Chainsaw,* she was an abused and alienated teen slasher fanatic, who secretly yearned for an orgy of bloodshed, even as she tried to stop the killings. The Jade we find here has mellowed; she hasn't watched a horror movie in years and is eager to leave her high school self behind.

Having established his setting and characters in the first installment, Jones allows us to spend time hanging out with Jade and her friends: gruff but tender-hearted Sheriff Hardy, wealthy but scarred former final girl Letha Mondragon, and Letha's new husband, in-over-his-head sheriff's deputy Banner Tompkins. (Banner and Jade wouldn't have given each other the time of day in high school; the way they hit it off now is a testament to their maturity). We also meet Jade's estranged mother, a broken soul living off a dwindling supply of golden memories.

Some of the reunions are more sinister. We see pervy janitor Rexall in the throes of grief, convinced his dead friend Tab (Jade's father) will eventually rise from the lake to take his revenge. We catch up with the ghost of lake witch Stacey Graves, the local legend responsible for much of the bloodshed in the first book.

82

And we get a supremely creepy conversation with institutionalized teen Ginger Baker, a scene that reads like Jones remaking *Exorcist III*.

Jade may have given up slashers, but the horror bug has spread in her absence. In the aftermath of the Lake Witch Murders, traumatized locals have committed themselves to learning the Gospel of the Slasher, with Jade's videotapes and essays ascending to the status of holy relics. And Jade, of course, will have to rediscover her inner Randy Meeks if she wants to survive.

Beyond the obvious references, Jones has an uncanny ability to re-create the feeling of *watching* a slasher movie. The dread and the jump scares, yes, but also the less tangible sensations. In *Chainsaw*, Jade's attitude mirrored the cognitive dissonance horror fans feel as we root for a victim to get away, while simultaneously hoping they get a machete to the skull. In *Reaper*, Jones exploits the subtle feeling of wrongness that permeates certain sequels.

For instance – you know how later entries in slasher franchises awkwardly introduce new characters to fill the void left by killed-off fan favourites? Here, Jade's effervescent "Slasher 101" mini-essays (extra credit assignments written for her beloved teacher) are replaced by similar missives by a young massacre survivor, addressed to the school's new history teacher. These essays are interesting, yes - but there's something off about them. The tone is calculating rather than joyful, and the relationship between student and teacher feels coercive rather than supportive.

But isn't that what sequels do? Hew close enough to the original to honour it, while differentiating themselves enough to keep the audience off-guard?

As Jones well knows. Because as much as his stories are in conversation with other works, they talk to each other, too. An early version of the Lake Witch can be found in his 2006 short story "Raphael." Jade's arc in *Chainsaw* mirrored his protagonist's fate in *Night of the Mannequins*. And *Reaper* includes a heartbreaking sequence that evokes the mythology of *The Only Good Indians*.

Jones also weaves in history, Dark Mill South's trail of bodies reflecting the psychic scars of colonialism. Speculation that this villain might have been influenced by historical atrocities against Indigenous people, or his own suffering in an Indian Boarding School, is uncomfortable but timely.

There's a subtle magical realism in *Don't Fear the Reaper*, implying a mystical throughline between seemingly unrelated events and characters. You can see it in the way Proofrock's historical tragedies feed into each other, not to mention the suggestion of kinship between Dark Mill South and Jade's abusive father (the real monster in her life). The fact that slasher movie rules are true in Proofrock isn't just a gimmick, but an assertion that fiction and reality aren't far off from each other.

Stephen Graham Jones is a literary writer obsessed with horror movies, whose encyclopedic knowledge of slasher lore is matched by his innate understanding of the genre's capacity for metaphor and symbolism. *My Heart is a Chainsaw* explored themes of alienation, community, and the stories we tell ourselves to survive. *In Don't Fear the Reaper*, Jones mines the sequel format to comment on the aftereffects of trauma, and how history doesn't just repeat, but mutates.

Madison McSweeney